PENGUIN BOOKS

THE DAY OF THE LOCUST
and
THE DREAM LIFE OF BALSO SNELL

Nathan Wallenstein Weinstein was born in 1903. He attended Brown University and from 1924 to 1931 he lived in
Paris, where he wrote *The Dream Life of Balso Snell*. On his
return to New York he managed a residential hotel and was
associate editor, with William Carlos Williams, of the
magazine *Contact*. *Miss Lonelyhearts* appeared in 1933, *A
Cool Million* in 1934 and *The Day of the Locust* in 1939. He
worked on film scripts in Hollywood for the last five years
of his life. He and his wife were tragically killed in a car
accident in 1940.

NATHANAEL WEST

THE DAY OF THE LOCUST

THE DREAM LIFE OF
BALSO SNELL

PENGUIN BOOKS

PENGUIN BOOKS

Published by the Penguin Group
Penguin Books Ltd, 80 Strand, London WC2R 0RL, England
Penguin Putnam Inc., 375 Hudson Street, New York, New York 10014, USA
Penguin Books Australia Ltd, 250 Camberwell Road, Camberwell, Victoria 3124, Australia
Penguin Books Canada Ltd, 10 Alcorn Avenue, Toronto, Ontario, Canada M4V 3B2
Penguin Books India (P) Ltd, 11 Community Centre, Panchsheel Park, New Delhi – 110 017, India
Penguin Books (NZ) Ltd, Cnr Rosedale and Airborne Roads, Albany, Auckland, New Zealand
Penguin Books (South Africa) (Pty) Ltd, 24 Sturdee Avenue, Rosebank 2196, South Africa

Penguin Books Ltd, Registered Offices: 80 Strand, London WC2R 0RL, England

www.penguin.com

The Day of the Locust first published in the USA 1939
The Dream Life of Balso Snell first published in the USA 1931
First published in Penguin Books in *The Collected Works of Nathanael West* 1975
Reissued in this edition 1991
Reprinted in Penguin Classics 2000
10

Printed in England by Clays Ltd, St Ives plc

ISBN-13: 978-0-141-18288-9

CONTENTS

The Day of the Locust

For LAURA

1

Around quitting time, Tod Hackett heard a great din on the road outside his office. The groan of leather mingled with the jangle of iron and over all beat the tattoo of a thousand hooves. He hurried to the window.

An army of cavalry and foot was passing. It moved like a mob; its lines broken, as though fleeing from some terrible defeat. The dolmans of the hussars, the heavy shakos of the guards, Hanoverian light horse, with their flat leather caps and flowing red plumes, were all jumbled together in bobbing disorder. Behind the cavalry came the infantry, a wild sea of waving sabretaches, sloped muskets, crossed shoulder belts and swinging cartridge boxes. Tod recognized the scarlet infantry of England with their white shoulder pads, the black infantry of the Duke of Brunswick, the French grenadiers with their enormous white gaiters, the Scotch with bare knees under plaid skirts.

While he watched, a little fat man, wearing a cork sunhelmet, polo shirt and knickers, darted around the corner of the building in pursuit of the army.

"Stage Nine—you bastards—Stage Nine!" he screamed through a small megaphone.

The cavalry put spur to their horses and the infantry broke into a dogtrot. The little man in the cork hat ran after them, shaking his fist and cursing.

Tod watched until they had disappeared behind half a Mississippi steamboat, then put away his pencils and drawing board, and left the office. On the sidewalk outside the studio he stood for a moment trying to decide whether to walk home or take a streetcar. He had been in Hollywood less than three months and still found it a very exciting place, but he was lazy and didn't like to walk. He decided to take the streetcar as far as Vine Street and walk the rest of the way.

A talent scout for National Films had brought Tod to the Coast after seeing some of his drawings in an exhibit of undergraduate work at the Yale School of Fine Arts. He had been hired by telegram. If the scout had met Tod, he probably wouldn't have sent him to Hollywood to learn set and costume designing. His large, sprawling body, his slow blue eyes and sloppy grin made him seem completely without talent, almost doltish in fact.

Yes, despite his appearance, he was really a very complicated young man with a whole set of personalities, one inside the other like a nest of Chinese boxes. And "The

Burning of Los Angeles," a picture he was soon to paint, definitely proved he had talent.

He left the car at Vine Street. As he walked along, he examined the evening crowd. A great many of the people wore sports clothes which were not really sports clothes. Their sweaters, knickers, slacks, blue flannel jackets with brass buttons were fancy dress. The fat lady in the yachting cap was going shopping, not boating; the man in the Norfolk jacket and Tyrolean hat was returning, not from a mountain, but an insurance office; and the girl in slacks and sneaks with a bandanna around her head had just left a switchboard, not a tennis court.

Scattered among these masquerades were people of a different type. Their clothing was somber and badly cut, bought from mail-order houses. While the others moved rapidly, darting into stores and cocktail bars, they loitered on the corners or stood with their backs to the shop windows and stared at everyone who passed. When their stare was returned, their eyes filled with hatred. At this time Tod knew very little about them except that they had come to California to die.

He was determined to learn much more. They were the people he felt he must paint. He would never again do a fat red barn, old stone wall or sturdy Nantucket fisherman. From the moment he had seen them, he had known that, despite his race, training and heritage, neither Winslow Homer nor Thomas Ryder could be his masters and he turned to Goya and Daumier.

He had learned this just in time. During his last year in art school, he had begun to think that he might give up painting completely. The pleasures he received from the problems of composition and color had decreased as his facility had increased and he had realized that he was going the way of all his classmates, toward illustration or mere handsomeness. When the Hollywood job had come along, he had grabbed it despite the arguments of his friends who were certain that he was selling out and would never paint again.

He reached the end of Vine Street and began the climb into Pinyon Canyon. Night had started to fall.

The edges of the trees burned with a pale violet light and their centers gradually turned from deep purple to black. The same violet piping, like a Neon tube, outlined the tops of the ugly, hump-backed hills and they were almost beautiful.

But not even the soft wash of dusk could help the houses. Only dynamite would be of any use against the Mexican ranch houses, Samoan huts, Mediterranean villas, Egyptian and Japanese temples, Swiss chalets, Tudor cottages, and every possible combination of these styles that lined the slopes of the canyon.

When he noticed that they were all of plaster, lath and paper, he was charitable and blamed their shape on the materials used. Steel, stone and brick curb a builder's fancy a little, forcing him to distribute his stresses and weights and to keep his corners plumb, but plaster and paper know no law, not even that of gravity.

On the corner of La Huerta Road was a miniature Rhine castle with tarpaper turrets pierced for archers. Next to it was a little highly colored shack with domes and minarets out of the *Arabian Nights*. Again he was charitable. Both houses were comic, but he didn't laugh. Their desire to startle was so eager and guileless.

It is hard to laugh at the need for beauty and romance, no matter how tasteless, even horrible, the results of that need are. But it is easy to sigh. Few things are sadder than the truly monstrous.

2

The house he lived in was a nondescript affair called the San Bernardino Arms. It was an oblong three stories high, the back and sides of which were of plain, unpainted stucco, broken by even rows of unadorned windows. The façade was the color of diluted mustard and its windows, all double, were framed by pink Moorish columns which supported turnip-shaped lintels.

His room was on the third floor, but he paused for a moment on the landing of the second. It was on that floor that Faye Greener lived, in 208. When someone laughed in one of the apartments he started guiltily and continued upstairs.

As he opened his door a card fluttered to the floor. "Honest Abe Kusich," it said in large type, then underneath in smaller italics were several endorsements, printed to look like press notices.

". . . *the Lloyds of Hollywood*"—*Stanley Rose*.

"*Abe's word is better than Morgan's bonds*"—*Gail Brenshaw*.

On the other side was a penciled message:

"Kingpin fourth, Solitair sixth. You can make some real dough on those nags."

After opening the window, he took off his jacket and lay down on the bed. Through the window he could see a square of enameled sky and a spray of eucalyptus. A light breeze stirred its long, narrow leaves, making them show first their green side, then their silver one.

He began to think of "Honest Abe Kusich" in order not to think of Faye Greener. He felt comfortable and wanted to remain that way.

Abe was an important figure in a set of lithographs called "The Dancers" on which Tod was working. He was

one of the dancers. Faye Greener was another and her
father, Harry, still another. They changed with each plate,
but the group of uneasy people who formed their audience
remained the same. They stood staring at the performers
in just the way that they stared at the masqueraders on
Vine Street. It was their stare that drove Abe and the
others to spin crazily and leap into the air with twisted
backs like hooked trout.

Despite the sincere indignation that Abe's grotesque de-
pravity aroused in him, he welcomed his company. The
little man excited him and in that way made him feel
certain of his need to paint.

He had first met Abe when he was living on Ivar Street,
in a hotel called the Chateau Mirabella. Another name for
Ivar Street was "Lysol Alley," and the Chateau was mainly
inhabited by hustlers, their managers, trainers and advance
agents.

In the morning its halls reeked of antiseptic. Tod didn't
like this odor. Moreover, the rent was high because it included police protection, a service for which he had no
need. He wanted to move, but inertia and the fact that he
didn't know where to go kept him in the Chateau until he
met Abe. The meeting was accidental.

He was on the way to his room late one night when he
saw what he supposed was a pile of soiled laundry lying in
front of the door across the hall from his own. Just as he
was passing it, the bundle moved and made a peculiar
noise. He struck a match, thinking it might be a dog
wrapped in a blanket. When the light flared up, he saw it
was a tiny man.

The match went out and he hastily lit another. It was a
male dwarf rolled up in a woman's flannel bathrobe. The
round thing at the end was his slightly hydrocephalic head.
A slow, choked snore bubbled from it.

The hall was cold and draughty. Tod decided to wake the man and stirred him with his toe. He groaned and opened his eyes.

"You oughtn't to sleep there."

"The hell you say," said the dwarf, closing his eyes again.

"You'll catch cold."

This friendly observation angered the little man still more.

"I want my clothes!" he bellowed.

The bottom of the door next to which he was lying filled with light. Tod decided to take a chance and knock. A few seconds later a woman opened it part way.

"What the hell do you want?" she demanded.

"There's a friend of yours out here who . . ."

Neither of them let him finish.

"So what!" she barked, slamming the door.

"Give me my clothes, you bitch!" roared the dwarf.

She opened the door again and began to hurl things into the hall. A jacket and trousers, a shirt, socks, shoes and underwear, a tie and hat followed each other through the air in rapid succession. With each article went a special curse.

Tod whistled with amazement.

"Some gal!"

"You bet," said the dwarf. "A lollapalooza—all slut and a yard wide."

He laughed at his own joke, using a high-pitched cackle more dwarflike than anything that had come from him so far, then struggled to his feet and arranged the voluminous robe so that he could walk without tripping. Tod helped him gather his scattered clothing.

"Say, mister," he asked, "could I dress in your place?"

Tod let him into his bathroom. While waiting for him to reappear, he couldn't help imagining what had happened in the woman's apartment. He began to feel sorry for having interfered. But when the dwarf came out wearing his hat, Tod felt better.

The little man's hat fixed almost everything. That year Tyrolean hats were being worn a great deal along Hollywood Boulevard and the dwarf's was a fine specimen. It was the proper magic green color and had a high, conical crown. There should have been a brass buckle on the front, but otherwise it was quite perfect.

The rest of his outfit didn't go well with the hat. Instead of shoes with long points and a leather apron, he wore a blue, double-breasted suit and a black shirt with a yellow tie. Instead of a crooked thorn stick, he carried a rolled copy of the *Daily Running Horse*.

"That's what I get for fooling with four-bit broads," he said by way of greeting.

Tod nodded and tried to concentrate on the green hat. His ready acquiescence seemed to irritate the little man.

"No quiff can give Abe Kusich the fingeroo and get away with it," he said bitterly. "Not when I can get her leg broke for twenty bucks and I got twenty."

He took out a thick billfold and shook it at Tod.

"So she thinks she can give me the fingeroo, hah? Well, let me tell . . ."

Tod broke in hastily.

"You're right, Mr. Kusich."

The dwarf came over to where Tod was sitting and for a moment Tod thought he was going to climb into his lap, but he only asked his name and shook hands. The little man had a powerful grip.

"Let me tell you something, Hackett, if you hadn't come along, I'da broke in the door. That dame thinks she can give me the fingeroo, but she's got another thinkola coming. But thanks anyway."

"Forget it."

"I don't forget nothing. I remember. I remember those who do me dirt and those who do me favors."

He wrinkled his brow and was silent for a moment.

"Listen," he finally said, "seeing as you helped me, I got to return it. I don't want anybody going around saying Abe Kusich owes him anything. So I'll tell you what. I'll give you a good one for the fifth at Caliente. You put a fiver on its nose and it'll get you twenty smackeroos. What I'm telling you is strictly correct."

Tod didn't know how to answer and his hesitation offended the little man.

"Would I give you a bum steer?" he demanded, scowling. "Would I?"

Tod walked toward the door to get rid of him.

"No," he said.

"Then why won't you bet, hah?"

"What's the name of the horse?" Tod asked, hoping to calm him.

The dwarf had followed him to the door, pulling the bathrobe after him by one sleeve. Hat and all, he came to a foot below Tod's belt.

"Tragopan. He's a certain, sure winner. I know the guy who owns him and he gave me the office."

"Is he a Greek?" Tod asked.

He was being pleasant in order to hide the attempt he was making to maneuver the dwarf through the door.

"Yeh, he's a Greek. Do you know him?"

"No."

"No?"

"No," said Tod with finality.

"Keep your drawers on," ordered the dwarf, "all I want to know is how you know he's a Greek if you don't know him?"

His eyes narrowed with suspicion and he clenched his fists.

Tod smiled to placate him.

"I just guessed it."

"You did?"

The dwarf hunched his shoulders as though he were going to pull a gun or throw a punch. Tod backed off and tried to explain.

"I guessed he was a Greek because Tragopan is a Greek word that means pheasant."

The dwarf was far from satisfied.

"How do you know what it means? You ain't a Greek?"

"No, but I know a few Greek words."

"So you're a wise guy, hah, a know-it-all."

He took a short step forward, moving on his toes, and Tod got set to block a punch.

"A college man, hah? Well, let me tell . . ."

His foot caught in the wrapper and he fell forward on his hands. He forgot Tod and cursed the bathrobe, then got started on the woman again.

"So she thinks she can give me the fingeroo."

He kept poking himself in the chest with his thumbs.

"Who gave her forty bucks for an abortion? Who? And another ten to go to the country for a rest that time. To a ranch I sent her. And who got her fiddle out of hock that time in Santa Monica? Who?"

"That's right," Tod said, getting ready to give him a quick shove through the door.

But he didn't have to shove him. The little man suddenly darted out of the room and ran down the hall, dragging the bathrobe after him.

A few days later, Tod went into a stationary store on Vine Street to buy a magazine. While he was looking through the rack, he felt a tug at the bottom of his jacket. It was Abe Kusich, the dwarf, again.

"How's things?" he demanded.

Tod was surprised to find that he was just as truculent

as he had been the other night. Later, when he got to know him better, he discovered that Abe's pugnacity was often a joke. When he used it on his friends, they played with him like one does with a growling puppy, staving off his mad rushes and then baiting him to rush again.

"Fair enough," Tod said, "but I think I'll move."

He had spent most of Sunday looking for a place to live and was full of the subject. The moment he mentioned it, however, he knew that he had made a mistake. He tried to end the matter by turning away, but the little man blocked him. He evidently considered himself an expert on the housing situation. After naming and discarding a dozen possibilities without a word from Tod, he finally hit on the San Bernardino Arms.

"That's the place for you, the San Berdoo. I live there, so I ought to know. The owner's strictly from hunger. Come on, I'll get you fixed up swell."

"I don't know, I . . ." Tod began.

The dwarf bridled instantly, and appeared to be mortally offended.

"I suppose it ain't good enough for you. Well, let me tell you something, you . . ."

Tod allowed himself to be bullied and went with the dwarf to Pinyon Canyon. The rooms in the San Berdoo were small and not very clean. He rented one without hesitation, however, when he saw Faye Greener in the hall.

3

Tod had fallen asleep. When he woke again, it was after eight o'clock. He took a bath and shaved, then dressed in front of the bureau mirror. He tried to watch his fingers as he fixed his collar and tie, but his eyes kept straying to the photograph that was pushed into the upper corner of the frame.

It was a picture of Faye Greener, a still from a two-reel farce in which she had worked as an extra. She had given him the photograph willingly enough, had even autographed it in a large, wild hand, "Affectionately yours, Faye Greener," but she refused his friendship, or, rather, insisted on keeping it impersonal. She had told him why. He had nothing to offer her, neither money nor looks, and she could only love a handsome man and would only let a wealthy man love her. Tod was a "good-hearted man," and she liked "good-hearted men," but only as friends. She wasn't hard-boiled. It was just that she put love on a special plane, where a man without money or looks couldn't move.

Tod grunted with annoyance as he turned to the photograph. In it she was wearing a harem costume, full Turkish trousers, breastplates and a monkey jacket, and lay stretched out on a silken divan. One hand held a beer bottle and the other a pewter stein.

He had gone all the way to Glendale to see her in that movie. It was about an American drummer who gets lost in the seraglio of a Damascus merchant and has a lot of fun with the female inmates. Faye played one of the dancing girls. She had only one line to speak, "Oh, Mr. Smith!" and spoke it badly.

She was a tall girl with wide, straight shoulders and long, swordlike legs. Her neck was long, too, and columnar. Her face was much fuller than the rest of her body would lead you to expect and much larger. It was a moon face, wide at the cheek bones and narrow at chin and brow. She wore her "platinum" hair long, letting it fall almost to her shoulders in back, but kept it away from her face and ears with a narrow blue ribbon that went under it and was tied on top of her head with a little bow.

She was supposed to look drunk and she did, but not with alcohol. She lay stretched out on the divan with her arms and legs spread, as though welcoming a lover, and her lips were parted in a heavy, sullen smile. She was supposed to look inviting, but the invitation wasn't to pleasure.

Tod lit a cigarette and inhaled with a nervous gasp. He started to fool with his tie again, but had to go back to the photograph.

Her invitation wasn't to pleasure, but to struggle, hard and sharp, closer to murder than to love. If you threw yourself on her, it would be like throwing yourself from the parapet of a skyscraper. You would do it with a scream. You couldn't expect to rise again. Your teeth would be driven into your skull like nails into a pine board and your back would be broken. You wouldn't even have time to sweat or close your eyes.

He managed to laugh at his language, but it wasn't a real laugh and nothing was destroyed by it.

If she would only let him, he would be glad to throw himself, no matter what the cost. But she wouldn't have him. She didn't love him and he couldn't further her career. She wasn't sentimental and she had no need for tenderness, even if he were capable of it.

When he had finished dressing, he hurried out of the room. He had promised to go to a party at Claude Estee's.

4

Claude was a successful screen writer who lived in a big house that was an exact reproduction of the old Dupuy mansion near Biloxi, Mississippi. When Tod came up the walk between the boxwood hedges, he greeted him from the enormous, two-story porch by doing the impersonation that went with the Southern colonial architecture. He teetered back and forth on his heels like a Civil War colonel and made believe he had a large belly.

He had no belly at all. He was a dried-up little man

with the rubbed features and stooped shoulders of a postal clerk. The shiny mohair coat and nondescript trousers of that official would have become him, but he was dressed, as always, elaborately. In the buttonhole of his brown jacket was a lemon flower. His trousers were of reddish Harris tweed with a hound tooth check and on his feet were a pair of magnificent, rust-colored blüchers. His shirt was ivory flannel and his knitted tie a red that was almost black.

While Tod mounted the steps to reach his outstretched hand, he shouted to the butler.

"Here, you black rascal! A mint julep."

A Chinese servant came running with a Scotch and soda.

After talking to Tod for a moment, Claude started him in the direction of Alice, his wife, who was at the other end of the porch.

"Don't run off," he whispered. "We're going to a sporting house."

Alice was sitting in a wicker swing with a woman named Mrs. Joan Schwartzen. When she asked him if he was playing any tennis, Mrs. Schwartzen interrupted her.

"How silly, batting an inoffensive ball across something that ought to be used to catch fish on account of millions are starving for a bite of herring."

"Joan's a female tennis champ," Alice explained.

Mrs. Schwartzen was a big girl with large hands and feet and square, bony shoulders. She had a pretty, eighteen-year-old face and a thirty-five-year-old neck that was veined and sinewy. Her deep sunburn, ruby colored with a slight blue tint, kept the contrast between her face and neck from being too startling.

"Well, I wish we were going to a brothel this minute," she said. "I adore them."

She turned to Tod and fluttered her eyelids.

"Don't you, Mr. Hackett?"

"That's right, Joan darling," Alice answered for him. "Nothing like a bagnio to set a fellow up. Hair of the dog that bit you."

"How dare you insult me!"

She stood up and took Tod's arm.

"Convoy me over there."

She pointed to the group of men with whom Claude was standing.

"For God's sake, convoy her," Alice said. "She thinks they're telling dirty stories."

Mrs. Schwartzen pushed right among them, dragging Tod after her.

"Are you talking smut?" she asked. "I adore smut."

They all laughed politely.

"No, shop," said someone.

"I don't believe it. I can tell from the beast in your voices. Go ahead, do say something obscene."

This time no one laughed.

Tod tried to disengage her arm, but she kept a firm grip on it. There was a moment of awkward silence, then the man she had interrupted tried to make a fresh start.

"The picture business is too humble," he said. "We ought to resent people like Coombes."

"That's right," said another man. "Guys like that come out here, make a lot of money, grouse all the time about the place, flop on their assignments, then go back East and tell dialect stories about producers they've never met."

"My God," Mrs. Schwartzen said to Tod in a loud, stagey whisper, "they *are* talking shop."

"Let's look for the man with the drinks," Tod said.

"No. Take me into the garden. Have you seen what's in the swimming pool?"

She pulled him along.

The air of the garden was heavy with the odor of

mimosa and honeysuckle. Through a slit in the blue serge sky poked a grained moon that looked like an enormous bone button. A little flagstone path, made narrow by its border of oleander, led to the edge of the sunken pool. On the bottom, near the deep end, he could see a heavy, black mass of some kind.

"What is it?" he asked.

She kicked a switch that was hidden at the base of a shrub and a row of submerged floodlights illuminated the green water. The thing was a dead horse, or, rather, a life-size, realistic reproduction of one. Its legs stuck up stiff and straight and it had an enormous, distended belly. Its hammerhead lay twisted to one side and from its mouth, which was set in an agonized grin, hung a heavy, black tongue.

"Isn't it marvelous!" exclaimed Mrs. Schwartzen, clapping her hands and jumping up and down excitedly like a little girl.

"What's it made of?"

"Then you weren't fooled? How impolite! It's rubber, of course. It cost lots of money."

"But why?"

"To amuse. We were looking at the pool one day and somebody, Jerry Appis, I think, said that it needed a dead horse on the bottom, so Alice got one. Don't you think it looks cute?"

"Very."

"You're just an old meanie. Think how happy the Estees must feel, showing it to people and listening to their merriment and their oh's and ah's of unconfined delight."

She stood on the edge of the pool and "ohed and ahed" rapidly several times in succession.

"Is it still there?" someone called.

Tod turned and saw two women and a man coming down the path.

"I think its belly's going to burst," Mrs. Schwartzen shouted to them gleefully.

"Goody," said the man, hurrying to look.

"But it's only full of air," said one of the women.

Mrs. Schwartzen made believe she was going to cry.

"You're just like that mean Mr. Hackett. You just won't let me cherish my illusions."

Tod was halfway to the house when she called after him. He waved but kept going.

The men with Claude were still talking shop.

"But how are you going to get rid of the illiterate mockies that run it? They've got a strangle hold on the industry. Maybe they're intellectual stumblebums, but they're damn good businessmen. Or at least they know how to go into receivership and come up with a gold watch in their teeth."

"They ought to put some of the millions they make back into the business again. Like Rockefeller does with his Foundation. People used to hate the Rockefellers, but now instead of hollering about their ill-gotten oil dough, everybody praises them for what the Foundation does. It's a swell stunt and pictures could do the same thing. Have a Cinema Foundation and make contributions to Science and Art. You know, give the racket a front."

Tod took Claude to one side to say good night, but he wouldn't let him go. He led him into the library and mixed two double Scotches. They sat down on the couch facing the fireplace.

"You haven't been to Audrey Jenning's place?" Claude asked.

"No, but I've heard tell of it."

"Then you've got to come along."

"I don't like pro-sport."

"We won't indulge in any. We're just going to see a movie."

"I get depressed."

"Not at Jenning's you won't. She makes vice attractive by skillful packaging. Her dive's a triumph of industrial design."

Tod liked to hear him talk. He was master of an involved comic rhetoric that permitted him to express his moral indignation and still keep his reputation for worldliness and wit.

Tod fed him another lead. "I don't care how much cellophane she wraps it in," he said—"nautch joints are depressing, like all places for deposit, banks, mail boxes, tombs, vending machines."

"Love is like a vending machine, eh? Not bad. You insert a coin and press home the lever. There's some mechanical activity inside the bowels of the device. You receive a small sweet, frown at yourself in the dirty mirror, adjust your hat, take a firm grip on your umbrella and walk away, trying to look as though nothing had happened. It's good, but it's not for pictures."

Tod played straight again.

"That's not it. I've been chasing a girl and it's like carrying something a little too large to conceal in your pocket, like a briefcase or a small valise. It's uncomfortable."

"I know, I know. It's always uncomfortable. First your right hand gets tired, then your left. You put the valise down and sit on it, but people are surprised and stop to stare at you, so you move on. You hide it behind a tree and hurry away, but someone finds it and runs after you to return it. It's a small valise when you leave home in the morning, cheap and with a bad handle, but by evening it's a trunk with brass corners and many foreign labels. I know. It's good, but it won't film. You've got to remember your audience. What about the barber in Purdue? He's been cutting hair all day and he's tired. He doesn't want to see some dope carrying a valise or fooling with a nickel machine. What the barber wants is amour and glamor."

The last part was for himself and he sighed heavily. He was about to begin again when the Chinese servant came in and said that the others were ready to leave for Mrs. Jenning's.

5

They started out in several cars. Tod rode in the front of the one Claude drove and as they went down Sunset Boulevard he described Mrs. Jenning for him. She had been a fairly prominent actress in the days of silent films, but sound made it impossible for her to get work. Instead of becoming an extra or a bit player like many other old stars, she had shown excellent business sense and had opened a callhouse. She wasn't vicious. Far from it. She ran her business just as other women run lending libraries, shrewdly and with taste.

None of the girls lived on the premises. You telephoned and she sent a girl over. The charge was thirty dollars for a single night of sport and Mrs. Jenning kept fifteen of it. Some people might think that fifty per cent is a high brokerage fee, but she really earned every cent of it. There was a big overhead. She maintained a beautiful house for the girls to wait in and a car and a chauffeur to deliver them to the clients.

Then, too, she had to move in the kind of society where she could make the right contacts. After all, not every man can afford thirty dollars. She permitted her girls to service only men of wealth and position, not to say taste and discretion. She was so particular that she insisted on meeting the prospective sportsman before servicing him. She had often said, and truthfully, that she would not let a girl of hers go to a man with whom she herself would not be willing to sleep.

And she was really cultured. All the most distinguished visitors considered it quite a lark to meet her. They were disappointed, however, when they discovered how refined she was. They wanted to talk about certain lively matters of universal interest, but she insisted on discussing Gertrude Stein and Juan Gris. No matter how hard the distinguished visitor tried, and some had been known to go to really great lengths, he could never find a flaw in her refinement or make a breach in her culture.

Claude was still using his peculiar rhetoric on Mrs. Jenning when she came to the door of her house to greet them.

"It's so nice to see you again," she said. "I was telling Mrs. Prince at tea only yesterday—the Estees are my favorite couple."

She was a handsome woman, smooth and buttery, with fair hair and a red complexion.

She led them into a small drawing room whose color scheme was violet, gray and rose. The Venetian blinds were rose, as was the ceiling, and the walls were covered with a pale gray paper that had a tiny, widely spaced flower design in violet. On one wall hung a silver screen, the kind that rolls up, and against the opposite wall, on each side of a cherrywood table, was a row of chairs covered with rose and gray, glazed chintz bound in violet piping. There was a small projection machine on the table and a young man in evening dress was fumbling with it.

She waved them to their seats. A waiter then came in and asked what they wanted to drink. When their orders had been taken and filled, she flipped the light switch and the young man started his machine. It whirred merrily, but he had trouble in getting it focused.

"What are we going to see first?" Mrs. Schwartzen asked.
"*Le Predicament de Marie.*"

"That sounds ducky."

"It's charming, utterly charming," said Mrs. Jenning.

"Yes," said the cameraman, who was still having trouble. "I love *Le Predicament de Marie*. It has a marvelous quality that is too exciting."

There was a long delay, during which he fussed desperately with his machine. Mrs. Schwartzen started to whistle and stamp her feet and the others joined in. They imitated a rowdy audience in the days of the nickelodeon.

"Get a move on, slow poke."

"What's your hurry? Here's your hat."

"Get a horse!"

"Get out and get under!"

The young man finally found the screen with his light beam and the film began.

LE PREDICAMENT DE MARIE

ou

LA BONNE DISTRAITE

Marie, the "bonne," was a buxom young girl in a tight-fitting black silk uniform with very short skirts. On her head was a tiny lace cap. In the first scene, she was shown serving dinner to a middle-class family in an oak-paneled dining room full of heavy, carved furniture. The family was very respectable and consisted of a bearded, frock-coated father, a mother with a whalebone collar and a cameo brooch, a tall, thin son with a long mustache and almost no chin and a little girl wearing a large bow in her hair and a crucifix on a gold chain around her neck.

After some low comedy with father's beard and the soup, the actors settled down seriously to their theme. It was evident that while the whole family desired Marie, she only desired the young girl. Using his napkin to hide his activities, the old man pinched Marie, the son tried to look down the neck of her dress and the mother patted her knee. Marie, for her part, surreptitiously fondled the child.

The scene changed to Marie's room. She undressed and got into a chiffon negligee, leaving on only her black silk stockings and high-heeled shoes. She was making an elaborate night toilet when the child entered. Marie took her on her lap and started to kiss her. There was a knock on the door. Consternation. She hid the child in the closet and let in the bearded father. He was suspicious and she had to accept his advances. He was embracing her when there was another knock. Again consternation and tableau. This time it was the mustachioed son. Marie hid the father under the bed. No sooner had the son begun to grow warm than there was another knock. Marie made him climb into a large blanket chest. The new caller was the lady of the house. She, too, was just settling down to work when there was another knock.

Who could it be? A telegram? A policeman? Frantically Marie counted the different hiding places. The whole family was present. She tiptoed to the door and listened.

"Who can it be that wishes to enter now?" read the title card.

And there the machine stuck. The young man in evening dress became as frantic as Marie. When he got it running again, there was a flash of light and the film whizzed through the apparatus until it had all run out.

"I'm sorry, extremely," he said. "I'll have to rewind."

"It's a frameup," someone yelled.

"Fake!"

"Cheat!"

"The old teaser routine!"

They stamped their feet and whistled.

Under cover of the mock riot, Tod sneaked out. He wanted to get some fresh air. The waiter, whom he found loitering in the hall, showed him to the patio in back of the house.

On his return, he peeked into the different rooms. In one of them he found a large number of miniature dogs in a curio cabinet. There were glass pointers, silver beagles, porcelain schnauzers, stone dachshunds, aluminum bull-dogs, onyx whippets, china bassets, wooden spaniels. Every recognized breed was represented and almost every material that could be sculptured, cast or carved.

While he was admiring the little figures, he heard a girl singing. He thought he recognized her voice and peeked into the hall. It was Mary Dove, one of Faye Greener's best friends.

Perhaps Faye also worked for Mrs. Jenning. If so, for thirty dollars . . .

He went back to see the rest of the film.

6

Tod's hope that he could end his trouble by paying a small fee didn't last long. When he got Claude to ask Mrs. Jenning about Faye, that lady said she had never heard of the girl. Claude then asked her to inquire through Mary Dove. A few days later she phoned him to say there was nothing doing. The girl wasn't available.

Tod wasn't really disappointed. He didn't want Faye that way, not at least while he still had a chance some other way. Lately, he had begun to think he had a good one. Harry, her father, was sick and that gave him an excuse for hanging around their apartment. He ran errands and kept the old man company. To repay his kindness, she permitted him the intimacies of a family friend. He hoped to deepen her gratitude and make it serious.

Apart from this purpose, he was interested in Harry and enjoyed visiting him. The old man was a clown and Tod had all the painter's usual love of clowns. But what was more important, he felt that his clownship was a clue to the people who stared (a painter's clue, that is—a clue in the form of a symbol), just as Faye's dreams were another.

He sat near Harry's bed and listened to his stories by the hour. Forty years in vaudeville and burlesque had provided him with an infinite number of them. As he put it, his life had consisted of a lightning series of "nip-ups," "high-gruesomes," "flying-W's" and "hundred-and-eights" done to escape a barrage of "exploding stoves." An "exploding stove" was any catastrophe, natural or human, from a flood in Medicine Hat, Wyoming, to an angry policeman in Moose Factory, Ontario.

When Harry had first begun his stage career, he had probably restricted his clowning to the boards, but now he clowned continuously. It was his sole method of defense. Most people, he had discovered, won't go out of their way to punish a clown.

He used a set of elegant gestures to accent the comedy of his bent, hopeless figure and wore a special costume, dressing like a banker, a cheap, unconvincing, imitation banker. The costume consisted of a greasy derby with an unusually high crown, a wing collar and polka dot four-in-hand, a shiny double-breasted jacket and gray-striped trousers. His outfit fooled no one, but then he didn't intend it to fool anyone. His slyness was of a different sort.

On the stage he was a complete failure and knew it. Yet he claimed to have once come very close to success. To prove how close, he made Tod read an old clipping from the theatrical section of the Sunday *Times*.

"BEDRAGGLED HARLEQUIN," it was headed.

"The commedia del' arte is not dead, but lives on in

Brooklyn, or was living there last week on the stage of the Oglethorpe Theatre in the person of one Harry Greener. Mr. Greener is of a troupe called 'The Flying Lings,' who, by the time this reaches you, have probably moved on to Mystic, Connecticut, or some other place more fitting than the borough of large families. If you have the time and really love the theatre, by all means seek out the Lings wherever they may be.

"Mr. Greener, the bedraggled Harlequin of our caption, is not bedraggled but clean, neat and sweet when he first comes on. By the time the Lings, four muscular Orientals, finish with him, however, he is plenty bedraggled. He is tattered and bloody, but still sweet.

"When Mr. Greener enters the trumpets are properly silent. Mama Ling is spinning a plate on the end of a stick held in her mouth, Papa Ling is doing cartwheels, Sister Ling is juggling fans and Sonny Ling is hanging from the proscenium arch by his pigtail. As he inspects his strenuous colleagues, Mr. Greener tries to hide his confusion under some much too obvious worldliness. He ventures to tickle Sister and receives a powerful kick in the belly in return for this innocent attention. Having been kicked, he is on familiar ground and begins to tell a dull joke. Father Ling sneaks up behind him and tosses him to Brother, who looks the other way. Mr. Greener lands on the back of his neck. He shows his mettle by finishing his dull story from a recumbent position. When he stands up, the audience, which failed to laugh at his joke, laughs at his limp, so he continues lame for the rest of the act.

"Mr. Greener begins another story, even longer and duller than his first. Just before he arrives at the gag line, the orchestra blares loudly and drowns him out. He is very patient and very brave. He begins again, but the orchestra will not let him finish. The pain that almost, not quite, thank God, crumples his stiff little figure would be unbearable if it were not obviously make-believe. It is gloriously funny.

"The finale is superb. While the Ling Family flies through the air, Mr. Greener, held to the ground by his sense of reality and his knowledge of gravitation, tries hard to make the audience think that he is neither surprised nor worried by the rocketing Orientals. It's familiar stuff, his hands signal, but his face denies this. As time goes on and no one is hurt, he regains his assurance. The acrobats ignore him, so he ignores the acrobats. His is the final victory; the applause is for him.

"My first thought was that some producer should put Mr. Greener into a big revue against a background of beautiful girls and glittering curtains. But my second was that this would be a mistake. I am afraid that Mr. Greener, like certain humble field plants which die when transferred to richer soil, had better be left to bloom in vaudeville against a background of ventriloquists and lady bicycle riders."

Harry had more than a dozen copies of this article, several on rag paper. After trying to get a job by inserting a small advertisement in *Variety* (". . . 'some producer should put Mr. Greener into a big revue . . .' The *Times*"), he had come to Hollywood, thinking to earn a living playing comedy bits in films. There proved to be little demand for his talents, however. As he himself put it, he "stank from hunger." To supplement his meager income from the studios, he peddled silver polish which he made in the bathroom of the apartment out of chalk, soap and yellow axle grease. When Faye wasn't at Central Casting, she took him around on his peddling trips in her Model T Ford. It was on their last expedition together that he had fallen sick.

It was on this trip that Faye acquired a new suitor by the name of Homer Simpson. About a week after Harry had taken to his bed, Tod met Homer for the first time. He was keeping the old man company when their conversation was interrupted by a light knock on the apartment door. Tod answered it and found a man standing in the hall with flowers for Faye and a bottle of port wine for her father.

Tod examined him eagerly. He didn't mean to be rude but at first glance this man seemed an exact model for the kind of person who comes to California to die, perfect in every detail down to fever eyes and unruly hands.

"My name is Homer Simpson," the man gasped, then shifted uneasily and patted his perfectly dry forehead with a folded handkerchief.

"Won't you come in?" Tod asked.

He shook his head heavily and thrust the wine and flowers at Tod. Before Tod could say anything, he had lumbered off.

Tod saw that he was mistaken. Homer Simpson was only physically the type. The men he meant were not shy.

He took the gifts in to Harry, who didn't seem at all surprised. He said Homer was one of his grateful customers.

"That Miracle Polish of mine sure does fetch 'em."

Later, when Faye came home and heard the story, she was very much amused. They both told Tod how they had happened to meet Homer, interrupting themselves and each other every few seconds to laugh.

The next thing Tod saw Homer staring at the apartment house from the shadow of a date palm on the opposite side of the street. He watched him for a few minutes, then called out a friendly greeting. Without replying, Homer ran away. On the next day and the one after, Tod again saw him lurking near the palm tree. He finally caught him by approaching the tree silently from the rear.

"Hello, Mr. Simpson," Tod said softly. "The Greeners were very grateful for your gift."

This time Simpson didn't move, perhaps because Tod had him backed against the tree.

"That's fine," he blurted out. "I was passing . . . I live up the street."

Tod managed to keep their conversation going for several minutes before he escaped again.

The next time Tod was able to approach him without the stalk. From then on, he responded very quickly to his advances. Sympathy, even of the most obvious sort, made him articulate, almost garrulous.

7

Tod was right about one thing at least. Like most of the people he was interested in, Homer was a Middle-Westerner. He came from a little town near Des Moines, Iowa, called Wayneville, where he had worked for twenty years in a hotel.

One day, while sitting in the park in the rain, he had caught cold and his cold developed into pneumonia. When he came out of the hospital, he found that the hotel had hired a new bookkeeper. They offered to take him on again, but his doctor advised him to go to California for a rest. The doctor had an authoritative manner, so Homer left Wayneville for the Coast.

After living for a week in a railroad hotel in Los Angeles, he rented a cottage in Pinyon Canyon. It was only the second house the real estate agent showed him, but he took it because he was tired and because the agent was a bully.

He rather liked the way the cottage was located. It was the last house in the canyon and the hills rose directly behind the garage. They were covered with lupines, Canterbury bells, poppies, and several varieties of large yellow daisy. There were also some scrub pines, Joshua and eucalyptus trees. The agent told him that he would see doves and plumed quail, but during all the time he lived there, he saw only a few large, black velvet spiders and a lizard. He grew very fond of the lizard.

The house was cheap because it was hard to rent. Most of the people who took cottages in that neighborhood wanted them to be "Spanish" and this one, so the agent claimed, was "Irish." Homer thought that the place looked kind of queer, but the agent insisted that it was cute.

The house was queer. It had an enormous and very crooked stone chimney, little dormer windows with big hoods and a thatched roof that came down very low on both sides of the front door. This door was of gumwood painted like fumed oak and it hung on enormous hinges. Although made by machine, the hinges had been carefully stamped to appear hand-forged. The same kind of care and skill had been used to make the roof thatching, which was not really straw but heavy fireproof paper colored and ribbed to look like straw.

The prevailing taste had been followed in the living room. It was "Spanish." The walls were pale orange flecked with pink and on them hung several silk armorial banners in red and gold. A big galleon stood on the mantelpiece. Its hull was plaster, its sails paper and its rigging wire. In the fireplace was a variety of cactus in gaily colored Mexican pots. Some of the plants were made of rubber and cork; others were real.

The room was lit by wall fixtures in the shape of galleons with pointed amber bulbs projecting from their decks. The table held a lamp with a paper shade, oiled to look like parchment, that had several more galleons painted on it. On each side of the windows red velvet draperies hung from black, double-headed spears.

The furniture consisted of a heavy couch that had fat monks for legs and was covered with faded red damask, and three swollen armchairs, also red. In the center of the room was a very long mahogany table. It was of the trestle type and studded with large-headed bronze nails. Beside each of the chairs was a small end table, the same color and design as the big one, but with a colored tile let into the top.

In the two small bedrooms still another style had been used. This the agent had called "New England." There was a spool bed made of iron grained like wood, a Windsor chair of the kind frequently seen in tea shops, and a Governor Winthrop dresser painted to look like unpainted pine. On the floor was a small hooked rug. On the wall facing the dresser was a colored etching of a snowbound Connecticut farmhouse, complete with wolf. Both of these rooms were exactly alike in every detail. Even the pictures were duplicates.

There was also a bathroom and a kitchen.

8

It took Homer only a few minutes to get settled in his new home. He unpacked his trunk, hung his two suits, both dark gray, in the closet of one of his bedrooms and put his shirts and underclothes into the dresser drawers. He made no attempt to rearrange the furniture.

After an aimless tour of the house and the yard, he sat down on the couch in the living room. He sat as though waiting for someone in the lobby of a hotel. He remained that way for almost half an hour without moving anything but his hands, then got up and went into the bedroom and sat down on the edge of the bed.

Although it was still early in the afternoon, he felt very

sleepy. He was afraid to stretch out and go to sleep. Not because he had bad dreams, but because it was so hard for him to wake again. When he fell asleep, he was always afraid that he would never get up.

But his fear wasn't as strong as his need. He got his alarm clock and set it for seven o'clock, then lay down with it next to his ear. Two hours later, it seemed like seconds to him, the alarm went off. The bell rang for a full minute before he began to work laboriously toward consciousness. The struggle was a hard one. He groaned. His head trembled and his feet shot out. Finally his eyes opened, then widened. Once more the victory was his.

He lay stretched out on the bed, collecting his senses and testing the different parts of his body. Every part was awake but his hands. They still slept. He was not surprised. They demanded special attention, had always demanded it. When he had been a child, he used to stick pins into them and once had even thrust them into a fire. Now he used only cold water.

He got out of bed in sections, like a poorly made automaton, and carried his hands into the bathroom. He turned on the cold water. When the basin was full, he plunged his hands in up to the wrists. They lay quietly on the bottom like a pair of strange aquatic animals. When they were thoroughly chilled and began to crawl about, he lifted them out and hid them in a towel.

He was cold. He ran hot water into the tub and began to undress, fumbling with the buttons of his clothing as though he were undressing a stranger. He was naked before the tub was full enough to get in and he sat down on a stool to wait. He kept his enormous hands folded quietly on his belly. Although absolutely still, they seemed curbed rather than resting.

Except for his hands, which belonged on a piece of monumental sculpture, and his small head, he was well proportioned. His muscles were large and round and he had a full, heavy chest. Yet there was something wrong. For all his size and shape, he looked neither strong nor fertile. He was like one of Picasso's great sterile athletes, who brood hopelessly on pink sand, staring at veined marble waves.

When the tub was full, he got in and sank down in the hot water. He grunted his comfort. But in another moment he would begin to remember, in just another moment. He tried to fool his memory by overwhelming it with tears and brought up the sobs that were always lurking uneasily in his chest. He cried softly at first, then harder. The sound he made was like that of a dog lapping gruel. He concentrated on how miserable and lonely he was, but it didn't work. The thing he was trying so desperately to avoid kept crowding into his mind.

One day when he was working in the hotel, a guest called Romola Martin had spoken to him in the elevator.

"Mr. Simpson, you're Mr. Simpson, the bookkeeper?"

"Yes."

"I'm in six-eleven."

She was small and childlike, with a quick, nervous manner. In her arms she coddled a package which obviously contained a square gin bottle.

"Yes," said Homer again, working against his natural instinct to be friendly. He knew that Miss Martin owed several weeks' rent and had heard the room clerk say she was a drunkard.

"Oh! . . ." the girl went on coquettishly, making obvious their difference in size, "I'm sorry you're worried about your bill, I . . ."

The intimacy of her tone embarrassed Homer.

"You'll have to speak to the manager," he rapped out, turning away.

He was trembling when he reached his office.

How bold the creature was! She was drunk, of course,

but not so drunk that she didn't know what she was doing. He hurriedly labeled his excitement disgust.

Soon afterwards the manager called and asked him to bring in Miss Martin's credit card. When he went into the manager's office, he found Miss Carlisle, the room clerk there. Homer listened to what the manager was saying to her.

"You roomed six-eleven?"

"I did, yes, sir."

"Why? She's obvious enough, isn't she?"

"Not when she's sober."

"Never mind that. We don't want her kind in this hotel."

"I'm sorry."

The manager turned to Homer and took the credit card he was holding.

"She owes thirty-one dollars," Homer said.

"She'll have to pay up and get out. I don't want her kind around here." He smiled. "Especially when they run up bills. Get her on the phone for me."

Homer asked the telephone operator for six-eleven and after a short time was told that the room didn't answer.

"She's in the house," he said. "I saw her in the elevator."

"I'll have the housekeeper look."

Homer was working on his books some minutes later when his phone rang. It was the manager again. He said that six-eleven had been reported in by the housekeeper and asked Homer to take her a bill.

"Tell her to pay up or get out," he said.

His first thought was to ask that Miss Carlisle be sent because he was busy, but he didn't dare to suggest it. While making out the bill, he began to realize how excited he was. It was terrifying. Little waves of sensation moved along his nerves and the base of his tongue tingled.

When he got off at the sixth floor, he felt almost gay.

His step was buoyant and he had completely forgotten his troublesome hands. He stopped at six-eleven and made as though to knock, then suddenly took fright and lowered his fist without touching the door.

He couldn't go through with it. They would have to send Miss Carlisle.

The housekeeper, who had been watching from the end of the hall, came up before he could escape.

"She doesn't answer," Homer said hurriedly.

"Did you knock hard enough? That slut is in there."

Before Homer could reply, she pounded on the door.

"Open up!" she shouted.

Homer heard someone move inside, then the door opened a few inches.

"Who is it, please?" a light voice asked.

"Mr. Simpson, the bookkeeper," he gasped.

"Come in, please."

The door opened a little wider and Homer went in without daring to look around at the housekeeper. He stumbled to the center of the room and stopped. At first he was conscious only of the heavy odor of alcohol and stale tobacco, but then underneath he smelled a metallic perfume. His eyes moved in a slow circle. On the floor was a litter of clothing, newspapers, magazines, and bottles. Miss Martin was huddled up on a corner of the bed. She was wearing a man's black silk dressing gown with light blue cuffs and lapel facings. Her close-cropped hair was the color and texture of straw and she looked like a little boy. Her youthfulness was heightened by her blue button eyes, pink button nose and red button mouth.

Homer was too busy with his growing excitement to speak or even think. He closed his eyes to tend it better, nursing carefully what he felt. He had to be careful, for if he went too fast, it might wither and then he would be cold again. It continued to grow.

"Go away, please, I'm drunk," Miss Martin said.

Homer neither moved nor spoke.

She suddenly began to sob. The coarse, broken sounds she made seemed to come from her stomach. She buried her face in her hands and pounded the floor with her feet.

Homer's feelings were so intense that his head bobbed stiffly on his neck like that of a toy Chinese dragon.

"I'm broke. I haven't any money. I haven't a dime. I'm broke, I tell you."

Homer pulled out his wallet and moved on the girl as though to strike her with it.

She cowered away from him and her sobs grew stronger.

He dropped the wallet in her lap and stood over her, not knowing what else to do. When she saw the wallet, she smiled, but continued sobbing.

"Sit down," she said.

He sat down on the bed beside her.

"You strange man," she said coyly. "I could kiss you for being so nice."

He caught her in his arms and hugged her. His suddenness frightened her and she tried to pull away, but he held on and began awkwardly to caress her. He was completely unconscious of what he was doing. He knew only that what he felt was marvelously sweet and that he had to make the sweetness carry through to the poor, sobbing woman.

Miss Martin's sobs grew less and soon stopped altogether. He could feel her fidget and gather strength.

The telephone rang.

"Don't answer it," she said, beginning to sob once more.

He pushed her away gently and stumbled to the telephone. It was Miss Carlisle.

"Are you all right?" she asked, "or shall we send for the cops?"

"All right," he said, hanging up.

It was all over. He couldn't go back to the bed.

Miss Martin laughed at his look of acute distress.

"Bring the gin, you enormous cow," she shouted gaily. "It's under the table."

He saw her stretch herself out in a way that couldn't be mistaken. He ran out of the room.

Now in California, he was crying because he had never seen Miss Martin again. The next day the manager had told him that he had done a good job and that she had paid up and checked out.

Homer tried to find her. There were two other hotels in Wayneville, small run-down houses, and he inquired at both of them. He also asked in the few rooming places, but with no success. She had left town.

He settled back into his regular routine, working ten hours, eating two, sleeping the rest. Then he caught cold and had been advised to come to California. He could easily afford not to work for a while. His father had left him about six thousand dollars and during the twenty years he had kept books in the hotel, he had saved at least ten more.

9

He got out of the tub, dried himself hurriedly with a rough towel, then went into the bedroom to dress. He felt even more stupid and washed out than usual. It was always like that. His emotions surged up in an enormous wave, curving and rearing, higher and higher, until it seemed as though the wave must carry everything before it. But the crash never came. Something always happened at the very top of the crest and the wave collapsed to run back like water down a drain, leaving, at the most, only the refuse of feeling.

It took him a long time to get all his clothing on. He stopped to rest after each garment with a desperation far out of proportion to the effort involved.

There was nothing to eat in the house and he had to go down to Hollywood Boulevard for food. He thought of waiting until morning, but then, although he was not hungry, decided against waiting. It was only eight o'clock and the trip would kill some time. If he just sat around, the temptation to go to sleep again would become irresistible.

The night was warm and very still. He started down hill, walking on the outer edge of the pavement. He hurried between lamp-posts, where the shadows were heaviest, and came to a full stop for a moment at every circle of light. By the time he reached the boulevard, he was fighting the desire to run. He stopped for several minutes on the corner to get his bearings. As he stood there, poised for flight, his fear made him seem almost graceful.

When several other people passed without paying any attention to him, he quieted down. He adjusted the collar of his coat and prepared to cross the street. Before he could take two steps someone called to him.

"Hey, you, mister."

It was a beggar who had spotted him from the shadow of a doorway. With the infallible instinct of his kind, he knew that Homer would be easy.

"Can you spare a nickel?"

"No," Homer said without conviction.

The beggar laughed and repeated his question, threateningly.

"A nickel, mister!"

He poked his hand into Homer's face.

Homer fumbled in his change pocket and dropped several coins on the sidewalk. While the man scrambled for them, he made his escape across the street.

The SunGold Market into which he turned was a large, brilliantly lit place. All the fixtures were chromium and the floors and walls were lined with white tile. Colored spotlights played on the showcases and counters, heightening the natural hues of the different foods. The oranges were bathed in red, the lemons in yellow, the fish in pale green, the steaks in rose and the eggs in ivory.

Homer went directly to the canned goods department and bought a can of mushroom soup and another of sardines. These and a half a pound of soda crackers would be enough for his supper.

Out on the street again with his parcel, he started to walk home. When he reached the corner that led to Pinyon Canyon and saw how steep and black the hill looked, he turned back along the lighted boulevard. He thought of waiting until someone else started up the hill, but finally took a taxicab.

10

Although Homer had nothing to do but prepare his scanty meals, he was not bored. Except for the Romola Martin incident and perhaps one or two other widely spaced events, the forty years of his life had been entirely without variety or excitement. As a bookkeeper, he had worked mechanically, totaling figures and making entries with the same impersonal detachment that he now opened cans of soup and made his bed.

Someone watching him go about his little cottage might have thought him sleep-walking or partially blind. His hands seemed to have a life and a will of their own. It was they who pulled the sheets tight and shaped the pillows.

One day, while opening a can of salmon for lunch, his thumb received a nasty cut. Although the wound must have hurt, the calm, slightly querulous expression he usually wore did not change. The wounded hand writhed about on the kitchen table until it was carried to the sink by its mate and bathed tenderly in hot water.

When not keeping house, he sat in the back yard, called the patio by the real estate agent, in an old broken deck chair. He went out to it immediately after breakfast to bake himself in the sun. In one of the closets he had found a tattered book and he held it in his lap without looking at it.

There was a much better view to be had in any direction other than the one he faced. By moving his chair in a quarter circle he could have seen a large part of the canyon twisting down to the city below. He never thought of making this shift. From where he sat, he saw the closed door of the garage and a patch of its shabby, tarpaper roof. In the foreground was a sooty, brick incinerator and a pile of rusty cans. A little to the right of them were the remains of a cactus garden in which a few ragged, tortured plants still survived.

One of these, a clump of thick, paddlelike blades, covered with ugly needles, was in bloom. From the tip of several of its topmost blades protruded a bright yellow flower, somewhat like a thistle blossom but coarser. No matter how hard the wind blew, its petals never trembled.

A lizard lived in a hole near the base of this plant. It was about five inches long and had a wedge-shaped head from which darted a fine, forked tongue. It earned a hard living catching the flies that strayed over to the cactus from the pile of cans.

The lizard was self-conscious and irritable, and Homer found it very amusing to watch. Whenever one of its elaborate stalks were foiled, it would shift about uneasily on its short legs and puff out its throat. Its coloring matched the cactus perfectly, but when it moved over to the cans where the flies were thick, it stood out very plainly. It would sit on the cactus by the hour without moving, then become impatient and start for the cans. The flies would spot it immediately and after several misses, it would sneak back sheepishly to its original post.

Homer was on the side of the flies. Whenever one of them, swinging too widely, would pass the cactus, he prayed silently for it to keep on going or turn back. If it lighted, he watched the lizard begin its stalk and held his breath until it had killed, hoping all the while that something would warn the fly. But no matter how much he wanted the fly to escape, he never thought of interfering, and was careful not to budge or make the slightest noise. Occasionally the lizard would miscalculate. When that happened Homer would laugh happily.

Between the sun, the lizard and the house, he was fairly well occupied. But whether he was happy or not it is hard to say. Probably he was neither, just as a plant is neither. He had memories to disturb him and a plant hasn't, but after the first bad night his memories were quiet.

11

He had been living this way for almost a month, when, one day, just as he was about to prepare his lunch, the door bell rang. He opened it and found a man standing on the step with a sample case in one hand and a derby hat in the other. Homer hurriedly shut the door again.

The bell continued to ring. He put his head out of the window nearest the door to order the fellow away, but the man bowed very politely and begged for a drink of water. Homer saw that he was old and tired and thought that he looked harmless. He got a bottle of water from the icebox, then opened the door and asked him in.

"The name, sir, is Harry Greener," the man announced in sing-song, stressing every other syllable.

Homer handed him a glass of water. He swallowed it quickly, then poured himself another.

"Much obliged," he said with an elaborate bow. "That was indeed refreshing."

Homer was astonished when he bowed again, did several quick jig steps, then let his derby hat roll down his arm. It fell to the floor. He stooped to retrieve it, straightening up with a jerk as though he had been kicked, then rubbed the seat of his trousers ruefully.

Homer understood that this was to amuse, so he laughed.

Harry thanked him by bowing again, but something went wrong. The exertion had been too much for him. His face blanched and he fumbled with his collar.

"A momentary indisposition," he murmured, wondering himself whether he was acting or sick.

"Sit down," Homer said.

But Harry wasn't through with his performance. He assumed a gallant smile and took a few unsteady steps toward the couch, then tripped himself. He examined the carpet indignantly, made believe he had found the object that had tripped him and kicked it away. He then limped to the couch and sat down with a whistling sigh like air escaping from a toy balloon.

Homer poured more water. Harry tried to stand up, but Homer pressed him back and made him drink sitting. He drank this glass as he had the other two, in quick gulps, then wiped his mouth with his handkerchief, imitating a man with a big mustache who had just drunk a glass of foamy beer.

"You are indeed kind, sir," he said. "Never fear, some day I'll repay you a thousandfold."

Homer clucked.

From his pocket Harry brought out a small can and held it out for him to take.

"Compliments of the house," he announced. "'Tis a box

of Miracle Solvent, the modern polish par excellence, the polish without peer or parallel, used by all the movie stars . . ."

He broke off his spiel with a trilling laugh.

Homer took the can.

"Thank you," he said, trying to appear grateful. "How much is it?"

"The ordinary price, the retail price, is fifty cents, but you can have it for the extraordinary price of a quarter, the wholesale price, the price I pay at the factory."

"A quarter?" asked Homer, habit for the moment having got the better of his timidity. "I can buy one twice that size for a quarter in the store."

Harry knew his man.

"Take it, take it for nothing," he said contemptuously.

Homer was tricked into protesting.

"I guess maybe this is a much better polish."

"No," said Harry, as though he were spurning a bribe. "Keep your money. I don't want it."

He laughed, this time bitterly.

Homer pulled out some change and offered it.

"Take it, please. You need it, I'm sure. I'll have two cans."

Harry had his man where he wanted him. He began to practice a variety of laughs, all of them theatrical, like a musician tuning up before a concert. He finally found the right one and let himself go. It was a victim's laugh.

"Please stop," Homer said.

But Harry couldn't stop. He was really sick. The last block that held him poised over the runway of self-pity had been knocked away and he was sliding down the chute, gaining momentum all the time. He jumped to his feet and began doing Harry Greener, poor Harry, honest Harry, well-meaning, humble, deserving, a good husband, a model father, a faithful Christian, a loyal friend.

Homer didn't appreciate the performance in the least. He was terrified and wondered whether to phone the police. But he did nothing. He just held up his hand for Harry to stop.

At the end of his pantomime, Harry stood with his head thrown back, clutching his throat, as though waiting for the curtain to fall. Homer poured him still another glass of water. But Harry wasn't finished. He bowed, sweeping his hat to his heart, then began again. He didn't get very far this time and had to gasp painfully for breath. Suddenly, like a mechanical toy that had been over-wound, something snapped inside of him and he began to spin through his entire repertoire. The effort was purely muscular, like the dance of a paralytic. He jigged, juggled his hat, made believe he had been kicked, tripped, and shook hands with himself. He went through it all in one dizzy spasm, then reeled to the couch and collapsed.

He lay on the couch with his eyes closed and his chest heaving. He was even more surprised than Homer. He had put on his performance four or five times already that day and nothing like this had happened. He was really sick.

"You've had a fit," Homer said when Harry opened his eyes.

As the minutes passed, Harry began to feel better and his confidence returned. He pushed all thought of sickness out of his mind and even went so far as to congratulate himself on having given the finest performance of his career. He should be able to get five dollars out of the big dope who was leaning over him.

"Have you any spirits in the house?" he asked weakly.

The grocer had sent Homer a bottle of port wine on approval and he went to get it. He filled a tumbler half full and handed it to Harry, who drank it in small sips, making the faces that usually go with medicine.

Speaking slowly, as though in great pain, he then asked Homer to bring in his sample case.

"It's on the doorstep. Somebody might steal it. The greater part of my small capital is invested in those cans of polish."

When Homer stepped outside to obey, he saw a girl near the curb. It was Faye Greener. She was looking at the house.

"Is my father in there?" she called out.

"Mr. Greener?"

She stamped her foot.

"Tell him to get a move on, damn it. I don't want to stay here all day."

"He's sick."

The girl turned away without giving any sign that she either heard or cared.

Homer took the sample case back into the house with him. He found Harry pouring himself another drink.

"Pretty fair stuff," he said, smacking his lips over it. "Pretty fair, all right, all right. Might I be so bold as to ask what you pay for a . . ."

Homer cut him short. He didn't approve of people who drank and wanted to get rid of him.

"Your daughter's outside," he said with as much firmness as he could muster. "She wants you."

Harry collapsed on the couch and began to breathe heavily. He was acting again.

"Don't tell her," he gasped. "Don't tell her how sick her old daddy is. She must never know."

Homer was shocked by his hypocrisy.

"You're better," he said as coldly as he could. "Why don't you go home?"

Harry smiled to show how offended and hurt he was by the heartless attitude of his host. When Homer said nothing, his smile became one expressing boundless courage. He got carefully to his feet, stood erect for a minute, then began to sway weakly and tumbled back on the couch.

"I'm faint," he groaned.

Once again he was surprised and frightened. He was faint.

"Get my daughter," he gasped.

Homer found her standing at the curb with her back to the house. When he called her, she whirled and came running toward him. He watched her for a second, then went in, leaving the door unlatched.

Faye burst into the room. She ignored Homer and went straight to the couch.

"Now what in hell's the matter?" she exploded.

"Darling daughter," he said. "I have been badly taken, and this gentleman has been kind enough to let me rest for a moment."

"He had a fit or something," Homer said.

She whirled around on him so suddenly that he was startled.

"How do you do?" she said, holding her hand forward and high up.

He shook it gingerly.

"Charmed," she said, when he mumbled something.

She spun around once more.

"It's my heart," Harry said. "I can't stand up."

The little performance he put on to sell polish was familiar to her and she knew that this wasn't part of it. When she turned to face Homer again, she looked quite tragic. Her head, instead of being held far back, now drooped forward.

"Please let him rest there," she said.

"Yes, of course."

Homer motioned her toward a chair, then got her a

match for her cigarette. He tried not to stare at her, but his good manners were wasted. Faye enjoyed being stared at.

He thought her extremely beautiful, but what affected him still more was her vitality. She was taut and vibrant. She was as shiny as a new spoon.

Although she was seventeen, she was dressed like a child of twelve in a white cotton dress with a blue sailor collar. Her long legs were bare and she had blue sandals on her feet.

"I'm so sorry," she said when Homer looked at her father again.

He made a motion with his hand to show that it was nothing.

"He has a vile heart, poor dear," she went on. "I've begged and begged him to go to a specialist, but you men are all alike."

"Yes, he ought to go to a doctor," Homer said.

Her odd mannerisms and artificial voice puzzled him. "What time is it?" she asked.

"About one o'clock."

She stood up suddenly and buried both her hands in her hair at the sides of her head, making it bunch at the top in a shiny ball.

"Oh," she gasped prettily, "and I had a luncheon date."

Still holding her hair, she turned at the waist without moving her legs, so that her snug dress twisted even tighter and Homer could see her dainty, arched ribs and little, dimpled belly. This elaborate gesture, like all her others, was so completely meaningless, almost formal, that she seemed a dancer rather than an affected actress.

"Do you like salmon salad?" Homer ventured to ask.

"Salmon sal-ahde?"

She seemed to be repeating the question to her stomach. The answer was yes.

"With plenty of mayonnaise, huh? I adore it."

"I was going to have some for lunch. I'll finish making it."

"Let me help."

They looked at Harry, who appeared to be asleep, then went into the kitchen. While he opened a can of salmon, she climbed on a chair and straddled it with her arms folded across the top of its back and rested her chin on her arms. Whenever he looked at her, she smiled intimately and tossed her pale, glittering hair first forward, then back.

Homer was excited and his hands worked quickly. He soon had a large bowl of salad ready. He set the table with his best cloth and his best silver and china.

"It makes me hungry just to look," she said.

The way she said this seemed to mean that it was Homer who made her hungry and he beamed at her. But before he had a chance to sit down, she was already eating. She buttered a slice of bread, covered the butter with sugar and took a big bite. Then she quickly smeared a gob of mayonnaise on the salmon and went to work. Just as he was about to sit down, she asked for something to drink. He poured her a glass of milk and stood watching her like a waiter. He was unaware of her rudeness.

As soon as she had gobbled up her salad, he brought her a large red apple. She ate the fruit more slowly, nibbling daintily, her smallest finger curled away from the rest of her hand. When she had finished it, she went back to the living room and Homer followed her.

Harry still lay as they had left him, stretched out on the sofa. The heavy noon-day sun hit directly on his face, beating down on him like a club. He hardly felt its blows, however. He was busy with the stabbing pain in his chest. He was so busy with himself that he had even stopped trying to plan how to get money out of the big dope.

Homer drew the window curtain to shade his face.

Harry didn't even notice. He was thinking about death. Faye bent over him. He saw, from under his partially closed eyelids, that she expected him to make a reassuring gesture. He refused. He examined the tragic expression that she had assumed and didn't like it. In a serious moment like this, her ham sorrow was insulting.

"Speak to me, Daddy," she begged.

She was baiting him without being aware of it.

"What the hell is this," he snarled, "a Tom show?"

His sudden fury scared her and she straightened up with a jerk. He didn't want to laugh, but a short bark escaped before he could stop it. He waited anxiously to see what would happen. When it didn't hurt he laughed again. He kept on, timidly at first, then with growing assurance. He laughed with his eyes closed and the sweat pouring down his brow. Faye knew only one way to stop him and that was to do something he hated as much as she hated his laughter. She began to sing.

"Jeepers Creepers!
Where'd ya get those peepers? . . ."

She trucked, jerking her buttocks and shaking her head from side to side.

Homer was amazed. He felt that the scene he was witnessing had been rehearsed. He was right. Their bitterest quarrels often took this form; he laughing, she singing.

"Jeepers Creepers!
Where'd ya get those eyes?
Gosh, all git up!
How'd they get so lit up?
Gosh all git . . ."

When Harry stopped, she stopped and flung herself into a chair. But Harry was only gathering strength for a final effort. He began again. This new laugh was not critical; it was horrible. When she was a child, he used to punish her with it. It was his masterpiece. There was a director who always called on him to give it when he was shooting a scene in an insane asylum or a haunted castle.

It began with a sharp, metallic crackle, like burning sticks, then gradually increased in volume until it became a rapid bark, then fell away again to an obscene chuckle. After a slight pause, it climbed until it was the nicker of a horse, then still higher to become a machinelike screech.

Faye listened helplessly with her head cocked on one side. Suddenly, she too laughed, not willingly, but fighting the sound.

"You bastard!" she yelled.

She leaped to the couch, grabbed him by the shoulders and tried to shake him quiet.

He kept laughing.

Homer moved as though he meant to pull her away, but he lost courage and was afraid to touch her. She was so naked under her skimpy dress.

"Miss Greener," he pleaded, making his big hands dance at the end of his arms. "Please, please . . ."

Harry couldn't stop laughing now. He pressed his belly with his hands, but the noise poured out of him. It had begun to hurt again.

Swinging her hand as though it held a hammer, she brought her fist down hard on his mouth. She hit him only once. He relaxed and was quiet.

"I had to do it," she said to Homer when he took her arm and led her away.

He guided her to a chair in the kitchen and shut the door. She continued to sob for a long time. He stood behind her chair, helplessly, watching the rhythmical heave of her shoulders. Several times his hands moved forward to comfort her, but he succeeded in curbing them.

When she was through crying, he handed her a napkin and she dried her face. The cloth was badly stained by her rouge and mascara.

"I've spoilt it," she said, keeping her face averted. "I'm very sorry."

"It was dirty," Homer said.

She took a compact from her pocket and looked at herself in its tiny mirror.

"I'm a fright."

She asked if she could use the bathroom and he showed her where it was. He then tiptoed into the living room to see Harry. The old man's breathing was noisy but regular and he seemed to be sleeping quietly. Homer put a cushion under his head without disturbing him and went back into the kitchen. He lit the stove and put the coffeepot on the flame, then sat down to wait for the girl to return. He heard her go into the living room. A few seconds later she came into the kitchen.

She hesitated apologetically in the doorway.

"Won't you have some coffee?"

Without waiting for her to reply, he poured a cup and moved the sugar and cream so that she could reach them.

"I had to do it," she said. "I just had to."

"That's all right."

To show her that it wasn't necessary to apologize, he busied himself at the sink.

"No, I had to," she insisted. "He laughs that way just to drive me wild. I can't stand it. I simply can't."

"Yes."

"He's crazy. We Greeners are all crazy."

She made this last statement as though there were merit in being crazy.

"He's pretty sick," Homer said, apologizing for her. "Maybe he had a sunstroke."

"No, he's crazy."

He put a plate of gingersnaps on the table and she ate them with her second cup of coffee. The dainty crunching sound she made chewing fascinated him.

When she remained quiet for several minutes, he turned from the sink to see if anything was wrong. She was smoking a cigarette and seemed lost in thought.

He tried to be gay.

"What are you thinking?" he said awkwardly, then felt foolish.

She sighed to show how dark and foreboding her thoughts were, but didn't reply.

"I'll bet you would like some candy," Homer said. "There isn't any in the house, but I could call the drugstore and they'd send it right over. Or some ice cream?"

"No, thanks, please."

"It's no trouble."

"My father isn't really a peddler," she said, abruptly. "He's an actor. I'm an actress. My mother was also an actress, a dancer. The theatre is in our blood."

"I haven't seen many shows. I . . ."

He broke off because he saw that she wasn't interested.

"I'm going to be a star some day," she announced as though daring him to contradict her.

"I'm sure you . . ."

"It's my life. It's the only thing in the whole world that I want."

"It's good to know what you want. I used to be a bookkeeper in a hotel, but . . ."

"If I'm not, I'll commit suicide."

She stood up and put her hands to her hair, opened her eyes wide and frowned.

"I don't go to shows very often," he apologized, pushing the gingersnaps toward her. "The lights hurt my eyes."

She laughed and took a cracker.

"I'll get fat."

"Oh, no."

"They say fat women are going to be popular next year. Do you think so? I don't. It's just publicity for Mae West."

He agreed with her.

She talked on and on, endlessly, about herself and about the picture business. He watched her, but didn't listen, and whenever she repeated a question in order to get a reply, he nodded his head without saying anything.

His hands began to bother him. He rubbed them against the edge of the table to relieve their itch, but it only stimulated them. When he clasped them behind his back, the strain became intolerable. They were hot and swollen. Using the dishes as an excuse, he held them under the cold water tap of the sink.

Faye was still talking when Harry appeared in the doorway. He leaned weakly against the door jamb. His nose was very red, but the rest of his face was drained white and he seemed to have grown too small for his clothing. He was smiling, however.

To Homer's amazement, they greeted each other as though nothing had happened.

"You okay now, Pop?"

"Fine and dandy, baby. Right as rain, fit as a fiddle and lively as a flea, as the feller says."

The nasal twang he used in imitation of a country yokel made Homer smile.

"Do you want something to eat?" he asked. "A glass of milk, maybe?"

"I could do with a snack."

Faye helped him over to the table. He tried to disguise how weak he was by doing an exaggerated Negro shuffle.

Homer opened a can of sardines and sliced some bread. Harry smacked his lips over the food, but ate slowly and with an effort.

"That hit the spot, all righty right," he said when he had finished.

He leaned back and fished a crumpled cigar butt out of his vest pocket. Faye lit it for him and he playfully blew a puff of smoke in her face.

"We'd better go, Daddy," she said.

"In a jiffy, child."

He turned to Homer.

"Nice place you've got here. Married?"

Faye tried to interfere.

"Dad!"

He ignored her.

"Bachelor, eh?"

"Yes."

"Well, well, a young fellow like you."

"I'm here for my health," Homer found it necessary to say.

"Don't answer his questions," Faye broke in.

"Now, now, daughter, I'm just being friendly like. I don't mean no harm."

He was still using an exaggerated backwoods accent. He spat dry into an imaginary spittoon and made believe he was shifting a cud of tobacco from cheek to cheek.

Homer thought his mimicry funny.

"I'd be lonesome and scared living alone in a big house like this," Harry went on. "Don't you ever get lonesome?"

Homer looked at Faye for his answer. She was frowning with annoyance.

"No," he said, to prevent Harry from repeating the uncomfortable question.

"No? Well, that's fine."

He blew several smoke rings at the ceiling and watched their behavior judiciously.

"Did you ever think of taking boarders?" he asked.

"Some nice, sociable folks, I mean. It'll bring in a little extra money and make things more homey."

Homer was indignant, but underneath his indignation lurked another idea, a very exciting one. He didn't know what to say.

Faye misunderstood his agitation.

"Cut it out, Dad," she exclaimed before Homer could reply. "You've been a big enough nuisance already."

"Just chinning," he protested innocently. "Just chewing the fat."

"Well, then, let's get going," she snapped.

"There's plenty of time," Homer said.

He wanted to add something stronger, but didn't have the courage. His hands were braver. When Faye shook good-bye, they clutched and refused to let go.

Faye laughed at their warm insistence.

"Thanks a million, Mr. Simpson," she said. "You've been very kind. Thanks for the lunch and for helping Daddy."

"We're very grateful," Harry chimed in. "You've done a Christian deed this day. God will reward you."

He had suddenly become very pious.

"Please look us up," Faye said. "We live close-by in the San Berdoo Apartments, about five blocks down the canyon. It's the big yellow house."

When Harry stood, he had to lean against the table for support. Faye and Homer each took him by the arm and helped him into the street. Homer held him erect, while Faye went to get their Ford which was parked across the street.

"We're forgetting your order of Miracle Salve," Harry said, "the polish without peer or parallel."

Homer found a dollar and slipped it into his hand. He hid the money quickly and tried to become businesslike.

"I'll leave the goods tomorrow."

"Yes, that'll be fine," Homer said. "I really need some silver polish."

Harry was angry because it hurt him to be patronized by a sucker. He made an attempt to re-establish what he considered to be their proper relationship by bowing ironically, but didn't get very far with the gesture and began to fumble with his Adam's apple. Homer helped him into the car and he slumped down in the seat beside Faye.

They drove off. She turned to wave, but Harry didn't even look back.

12

Homer spent the rest of the afternoon in the broken deck chair. The lizard was on the cactus, but he took little interest in its hunting. His hands kept his thoughts busy. They trembled and jerked, as though troubled by dreams. To hold them still, he clasped them together. Their fingers twined like a tangle of thighs in miniature. He snatched them apart and sat on them.

When the days passed and he couldn't forget Faye, he began to grow frightened. He somehow knew that his only defense was chastity, that it served him, like the shell of a tortoise, as both spine and armor. He couldn't shed it even in thought. If he did, he would be destroyed.

He was right. There are men who can lust with parts of themselves. Only their brain or their hearts burn and then not completely. There are others, still more fortunate, who are like the filaments of an incandescent lamp. They burn fiercely, yet nothing is destroyed. But in Homer's case it would be like dropping a spark into a barn full of hay. He had escaped in the Romola Martin incident, but he wouldn't escape again. Then, for one thing, he had had his job in the hotel, a daily all-day task that protected him by tiring him, but now he had nothing.

His thoughts frightened him and he bolted into the house, hoping to leave them behind like a hat. He ran into his bedroom and threw himself down on the bed. He was simple enough to believe that people don't think while asleep.

In his troubled state, even this delusion was denied him and he was unable to fall asleep. He closed his eyes and tried to make himself drowsy. The approach to sleep which had once been automatic had somehow become a long, shining tunnel. Sleep was at the far end of it, a soft bit of shadow in the hard glare. He couldn't run, only crawl toward the black patch. Just as he was about to give up, habit came to his rescue. It collapsed the shining tunnel and hurled him into the shadow.

When he awoke it was without a struggle. He tried to fall asleep once more, but this time couldn't even find the tunnel. He was thoroughly awake. He tried to think of how very tired he was, but he wasn't tired. He felt more alive than he had at any time since Romola Martin.

Outside a few birds still sang intermittently, starting and breaking off, as though sorry to acknowledge the end of another day. He thought that he heard the lisp of silk against silk, but it was only the wind playing in the trees. How empty the house was! He tried to fill it by singing.

"Oh, say can you see,
By the dawn's early light . . ."

It was the only song he knew. He thought of buying a victrola or a radio. He knew, however, that he would buy neither. This fact made him very sad. It was a pleasant sadness, very sweet and calm.

But he couldn't let well enough alone. He was impatient

and began to prod at his sadness, hoping to make it acute and so still more pleasant. He had been getting pamphlets in the mail from a travel bureau and he thought of the trips he would never take. Mexico was only a few hundred miles away. Boats left daily for Hawaii.

His sadness turned to anguish before he knew it and became sour. He was miserable again. He began to cry.

Only those who still have hope can benefit from tears. When they finish, they feel better. But to those without hope, like Homer, whose anguish is basic and permanent, no good comes from crying. Nothing changes for them. They usually know this, but still can't help crying.

Homer was lucky. He cried himself to sleep.

But he awoke again in the morning with Faye uppermost in his mind. He bathed, ate breakfast and sat in his deck chair. In the afternoon, he decided to go for a walk. There was only one way for him to go and that led past the San Bernardino Apartments.

Some time during his long sleep he had given up the battle. When he came to the apartment house, he peered into the amber-lit hallway and read the Greener card on the letter box, then turned and went home. On the next night, he repeated the trip, carrying a gift of flowers and wine.

13

Harry Greener's condition didn't improve. He remained in bed, staring at the ceiling with his hands folded on his chest.

Tod went to see him almost every night. There were usually other guests. Sometimes Abe Kusich, sometimes Anna and Annabelle Lee, a sister act of the nineteen-tens, more often the four Gingos, a family of performing Eskimos from Point Barrow, Alaska.

If Harry were asleep or there were visitors, Faye usually invited Tod into her room for a talk. His interest in her grew despite the things she said and he continued to find her very exciting. Had any other girl been so affected, he would have thought her intolerable. Faye's affectations, however, were so completely artificial that he found them charming.

Being with her was like being backstage during an amateurish, ridiculous play. From in front, the stupid lines and grotesque situations would have made him squirm with annoyance, but because he saw the perspiring stage-hands and the wires that held up the tawdry summerhouse with its tangle of paper flowers, he accepted everything and was anxious for it to succeed.

He found still another way to excuse her. He believed that while she often recognized the falseness of an attitude, she persisted in it because she didn't know how to be simpler or more honest. She was an actress who had learned from bad models in a bad school.

Yet Faye did have some critical ability, almost enough to recognize the ridiculous. He had often seen her laugh at herself. What was more, he had even seen her laugh at her dreams.

One evening they talked about what she did with herself when she wasn't working as an extra. She told him that she often spent the whole day making up stories. She laughed as she said it. When he questioned her, she described her method quite willingly.

She would get some music on the radio, then lie down on her bed and shut her eyes. She had a large assortment of stories to choose from. After getting herself in the right mood, she would go over them in her mind, as though they were a pack of cards, discarding one after another until she found the one that suited. On some days, she would run through the whole pack without making a choice. When that happened, she would either go to Vine Street for an ice cream soda or, if she was broke, thumb over the pack again and force herself to choose.

While she admitted that her method was too mechanical for the best results and that it was better to slip into a dream naturally, she said that any dream was better than no dream and beggars couldn't be choosers. She hadn't exactly said this, but he was able to understand it from what she did say. He thought it important that she smiled while telling him, not with embarrassment, but critically. However, her critical powers ended there. She only smiled at the mechanics.

The first time he had ever heard one of her dreams was late at night in her bedroom. About half an hour earlier, she had knocked on his door and had asked him to come and help her with Harry because she thought he was dying. His noisy breathing, which she had taken for the death rattle, had awakened her and she was badly frightened. Tod put on his bathrobe and followed her downstairs. When he got to the apartment, Harry had managed to clear his throat and his breathing had become quiet again.

She invited him into her room for a smoke. She sat on the bed and he sat beside her. She was wearing an old beach robe of white toweling over her pajamas and it was very becoming.

He wanted to beg her for a kiss but was afraid, not because she would refuse, but because she would insist on making it meaningless. To flatter her, he commented on her appearance. He did a bad job of it. He was incapable of direct flattery and got bogged down in a much too roundabout observation. She didn't listen and he broke off feeling like an idiot.

"I've got a swell idea," she said suddenly. "An idea how we can make some real money."

He made another attempt to flatter her. This time by assuming an attitude of serious interest.

"You're educated," she said. "Well, I've got some swell ideas for pictures. All you got to do is write them up and then we'll sell them to the studios."

He agreed and she described her plan. It was very vague until she came to what she considered would be its results, then she went into concrete details. As soon as they had sold one story, she would give him another. They would make loads and loads of money. Of course she wouldn't give up acting, even if she was a big success as a writer, because acting was her life.

He realized as she went on that she was manufacturing another dream to add to her already very thick pack. When she finally got through spending the money, he asked her to tell him the idea he was to "write up," keeping all trace of irony out of his voice.

On the wall of the room beyond the foot of her bed was a large photograph that must have once been used in the lobby of a theatre to advertise a Tarzan picture. It showed a beautiful young man with magnificent muscles, wearing only a narrow loin cloth, who was ardently squeezing a slim girl in a torn riding habit. They stood in a jungle clearing and all around the pair writhed great vines loaded with fat orchids. When she told her story, he knew that this photograph had a lot to do with inspiring it.

A young girl is cruising on her father's yacht in the South Seas. She is engaged to marry a Russian count, who is tall, thin and old, but with beautiful manners. He is on the yacht, too, and keeps begging her to name the day. But she is spoiled and won't do it. Maybe she became engaged to him in order to spite another man. She becomes interested in a young sailor who is far below her in station, but very handsome. She flirts with him because she is bored. The sailor refuses to be toyed with no matter how

much money she's got and tells her that he only takes
orders from the captain and to go back to her foreigner.
She gets sore as hell and threatens to have him fired, but
he only laughs at her. How can he be fired in the middle
of the ocean? She falls in love with him, although maybe
she doesn't realize it herself, because he is the first man
who has ever said no to one of her whims and because
he is so handsome. Then there is a big storm and the
yacht is wrecked near an island. Everybody is drowned,
but she manages to swim to shore. She makes herself a hut
of boughs and lives on fish and fruit. It's the tropics. One
morning, while she is bathing naked in a brook, a big
snake grabs her. She struggles but the snake is too strong
for her and it looks like curtains. But the sailor, who has
been watching her from behind some bushes, leaps to her
rescue. He fights the snake for her and wins.

Tod was to go on from there. He asked her how she
thought the picture should end, but she seemed to have lost
interest. He insisted on hearing, however.

"Well, he marries her, of course, and they're rescued.
First they're rescued and then they're married, I mean.
Maybe he turns out to be a rich boy who is being a sailor
just for the adventure of it, or something like that. You
can work it out easy enough."

"It's sure-fire," Tod said earnestly, staring at her wet
lips and the tiny point of her tongue which she kept moving
between them.

"I've got just hundreds and hundreds more."

He didn't say anything and her manner changed. While
telling the story, she had been full of surface animation
and her hands and face were alive with little illustrative
grimaces and gestures. But now her excitement narrowed
and became deeper and its play internal. He guessed
that she must be thumbing over her pack and that she
would soon select another card to show him.

He had often seen her like this, but had never before understood it. All these little stories, these little daydreams of hers, were what gave such extraordinary color and mystery to her movements. She seemed always to be struggling in their soft grasp as though she were trying to run in a swamp. As he watched her, he felt sure that her lips must taste of blood and salt and that there must be a delicious weakness in her legs. His impulse wasn't to aid her to get free, but to throw her down in the soft, warm mud and to keep her there.

He expressed some of his desire by a grunt. If he only had the courage to throw himself on her. Nothing less violent than rape would do. The sensation he felt was like that he got when holding an egg in his hand. Not that she was fragile or even seemed fragile. It wasn't that. It was her completeness, her egglike self-sufficiency, that made him want to crush her.

But he did nothing and she began to talk again.

"I've got another swell idea that I want to tell you. Maybe you had better write this one up first. It's a backstage story and they're making a lot of them this year."

She told him about a young chorus girl who gets her big chance when the star of the show falls sick. It was a familiar version of the Cinderella theme, but her technique was much different from the one she had used for the South Sea tale. Although the events she described were miraculous, her description of them was realistic. The effect was similar to that obtained by the artists of the Middle Ages, who, when doing a subject like the raising of Lazarus from the dead or Christ walking on water, were careful to keep all the details intensely realistic. She, like them, seemed to think that fantasy could be made plausible by a humdrum technique.

"I like that one, too," he said when she had finished.

"Think them over and do the one that has the best chance."

She was dismissing him and if he didn't act at once the opportunity would be gone. He started to lean toward her, but she caught his meaning and stood up. She took his arm with affectionate brusqueness—they were now business partners—and guided him to the door.

In the hall, when she thanked him for coming down and apologized for having disturbed him, he tried again. She seemed to melt a little and he reached for her. She kissed him willingly enough, but when he tried to extend the caress, she tore free.

"Whoa there, palsy-walsy," she laughed. "Mamma spank."

He started for the stairs.

"Good-bye now," she called after him, then laughed again.

He barely heard her. He was thinking of the drawings he had made of her and of the new one he would do as soon as he got to his room.

In "The Burning of Los Angeles" Faye is the naked girl in the left foreground being chased by the group of men and women who have separated from the main body of the mob. One of the women is about to hurl a rock at her to bring her down. She is running with her eyes closed and a strange half-smile on her lips. Despite the dreamy repose of her face, her body is straining to hurl her along at top speed. The only explanation for this contrast is that she is enjoying the release that wild flight gives in much the same way that a game bird must when, after hiding for several tense minutes, it bursts from cover in complete, unthinking panic.

14

Tod had other and more successful rivals than Homer Simpson. One of the most important was a young man called Earle Shoop.

Earle was a cowboy from a small town in Arizona. He worked occasionally in horse-operas and spent the rest of his time in front of a saddlery store on Sunset Boulevard. In the window of this store was an enormous Mexican saddle covered with carved silver, and around it was arranged a large collection of torture instruments. Among other things there were fancy, braided quirts, spurs with great spiked wheels, and double bits that looked as though they could break a horse's jaw without trouble. Across the back of the window ran a low shelf on which was a row of boots, some black, some red and some a pale yellow. All of the boots had scalloped tops and very high heels.

Earle always stood with his back to the window, his eyes fixed on a sign on the roof of a one-story building across the street that read: "Malted Milks Too Thick For A Straw." Regularly, twice every hour, he pulled a sack of tobacco and a sheaf of papers from his shirt pocket and rolled a cigarette. Then he tightened the cloth of his trousers by lifting his knee and struck a match along the underside of his thigh.

He was over six feet tall. The big Stetson hat he wore added five inches more to his height and the heels of his boots still another three. His polelike appearance was further exaggerated by the narrowness of his shoulders and by his lack of either hips or buttocks. The years he had spent in the saddle had not made him bowlegged. In fact his legs were so straight that his dungarees, bleached very light blue by the sun and much washing, hung down without a wrinkle, as though they were empty.

Tod could see why Faye thought him handsome. He had a two-dimensional face that a talented child might have drawn with a ruler and a compass. His chin was perfectly round and his eyes, which were wide apart, were also round. His thin mouth ran at right angles to his straight, perpendicular nose. His reddish tan complexion was the same color from hairline to throat, as though washed in by an expert, and it completed his resemblance to a mechanical drawing.

Tod had told Faye that Earle was a dull fool. She agreed laughing, but then said that he was "criminally handsome," an expression she had picked up in the chatter column of a trade paper.

Meeting her on the stairs one night, Tod asked if she would go to dinner with him.

"I can't. I've got a date. But you can come along."

"With Earle?"

"Yes, with Earle," she repeated, mimicking his annoyance.

"No, thanks."

She misunderstood, perhaps on purpose, and said, "He'll treat this time."

Earle was always broke and whenever Tod went with them he was the one who paid.

"That isn't it, and you damn well know it."

"Oh, isn't it?" she asked archly, then, absolutely sure of herself, added, "Meet us at Hodge's around five."

Hodge's was the saddlery store. When Tod got there, he found Earle Shoop at his usual post, just standing and just looking at the sign across the street. He had on his ten-gallon hat and his high-heeled boots. Neatly folded over his left arm was a dark gray jacket. His shirt was navy-blue cotton with large polka dots, each the size of a dime. The sleeves of his shirt were not rolled, but pulled to the middle of his forearm and held there by a pair of fancy, rose armbands. His hands were the same clean reddish tan as his face.

"Lo, thar," was the way he returned Tod's salute.

Tod found his Western accent amusing. The first time he had heard it, he had replied, "Lo, thar, stranger," and had been surprised to discover that Earle didn't know he was being kidded. Even when Tod talked about "cayuses," "mean hombres" and "rustlers," Earle took him seriously.

"Howdy, partner," Tod said.

Next to Earle was another Westerner in a big hat and boots, sitting on his heels and chewing vigorously on a little twig. Close behind him was a battered paper valise held together by heavy rope tied with professional-looking knots.

Soon after Tod arrived a third man came along. He made a thorough examination of the merchandise in the window, then turned and began to stare across the street like the other two.

He was middle-aged and looked like an exercise boy from a racing stable. His face was completely covered with a fine mesh of wrinkles, as though he had been sleeping with it pressed against a roll of rabbit wire. He was very shabby and had probably sold his big hat, but he still had his boots.

"Lo, boys," he said.

"Lo, Hink," said the man with the paper valise.

Tod didn't know whether he was included in the greetng, but took a chance and replied.

"Howdy."

Hink prodded the valise with his toe.

"Goin' some place, Calvin?" he asked.

"Azusa, there's a rodeo."

"Who's running it?"

"A fellow calls himself 'Badlands Jack.' "

"That grifter! . . . You goin', Earle?"

"Nope."

"I gotta eat," said Calvin.

Hink carefully considered all the information he had received before speaking again.

"Mono's makin' a new Buck Stevens," he said. "Will Ferris told me they'd use more than forty riders."

Calvin turned and looked up at Earle.

"Still got the piebald vest?" he asked slyly.

"Why?"

"It'll cinch you a job as a road agent."

Tod understood that this was a joke of some sort because Calvin and Hink chuckled and slapped their thighs loudly while Earle frowned.

There was another long silence, then Calvin spoke again.

"Ain't your old man still got some cows?" he asked Earle.

But Earle was wary this time and refused to answer.

Calvin winked at Tod, slowly and elaborately, contorting one whole side of his face.

"That's right, Earle," Hink said. "Your old man's still got some stock. Why don't you go home?"

They couldn't get a rise out of Earle, so Calvin answered the question.

"He dassint. He got caught in a sheep car with a pair of rubber boots on."

It was another joke. Calvin and Hink slapped their thighs and laughed, but Tod could see that they were waiting for something else. Earle, suddenly, without even shifting his weight, shot his foot out and kicked Calvin solidly in the rump. This was the real point of the joke. They were delighted by Earle's fury. Tod also laughed. The way Earle had gone from apathy to action without the usual transition was funny. The seriousness of his violence was even funnier.

A little while later, Faye drove by in her battered Ford

touring car and pulled into the curb some twenty feet away. Calvin and Hink waved, but Earle didn't budge. He took his time, as befitted his dignity. Not until she tooted her horn did he move. Tod followed a short distance behind him.

"Hi, cowboy," said Faye gaily.

"Lo, honey," he drawled, removing his hat carefully and replacing it with even greater care.

Faye smiled at Tod and motioned for them both to climb in. Tod got in the back. Earle unfolded the jacket he was carrying, slapped it a few times to remove the wrinkles, then put it on and adjusted its collar and shaped the roll of its lapels. He then climbed in beside Faye.

She started the car with a jerk. When she reached LaBrea, she turned right to Hollywood Boulevard and then left along it. Tod could see that she was watching Earle out of the corner of her eye and that he was preparing to speak.

"Get going," she said, trying to hurry him. "What is it?"

"Looka here, honey, I ain't got any dough for supper."

She was very much put out.

"But I told Tod we'd treat him. He's treated us enough times."

"That's all right," Tod interposed. "Next time'll do. I've got plenty of money."

"No, damn it," she said without looking around. "I'm sick of it."

She pulled into the curb and slammed on the brakes.

"It's always the same story," she said to Earle.

He adjusted his hat, his collar and his sleeves, then spoke.

"We've got some grub at camp."

"Beans, I suppose."

"Nope."

She prodded him.

"Well, what've you got?"

"Mig and me's set some traps."

Faye laughed.

"Rat traps, eh? We're going to eat rats."

Earle didn't say anything.

"Listen, you big, strong, silent dope," she said, "either make sense, or God damn it, get out of this car."

"They're quail traps," he said without the slightest change in his wooden, formal manner.

She ignored his explanation.

"Talking to you is like pulling teeth. You wear me out."

Tod knew that there was no hope for him in this quarrel. He had heard it all before.

"I didn't mean nothing," Earle said. "I was only funning. I wouldn't feed you rats."

She slammed off the emergency brake and started the car again. At Zacarias Street, she turned into the hills. After climbing steadily for a quarter of a mile, she reached a dirt road and followed it to its end. They all climbed out, Earle helping Faye.

"Give me a kiss," she said, smiling her forgiveness.

He took his hat off ceremoniously and placed it on the hood of the car, then wrapped his long arms around her. They paid no attention to Tod, who was standing off to one side watching them. He saw Earle close his eyes and pucker up his lips like a little boy. But there was nothing boyish about what he did to her. When she had had as much as she wanted, she pushed him away.

"You, too?" she called gaily to Tod, who had turned his back.

"Oh, some other time," he replied, imitating her casualness.

She laughed, then took out a compact and began to fix her mouth. When she was ready, they started along a little path that was a continuation of the dirt road. Earle led, Faye came next and Tod brought up the rear.

It was full spring. The path ran along the bottom of a narrow canyon and wherever weeds could get a purchase in its steep banks they flowered in purple, blue and yellow. Orange poppies bordered the path. Their petals were wrinkled like crepe and their leaves were heavy with talcumlike dust.

They climbed until they reached another canyon. This one was sterile, but its bare ground and jagged rocks were even more brilliantly colored than the flowers of the first. The path was silver, grained with streaks of rose-gray, and the walls of the canyon were turquoise, mauve, chocolate and lavender. The air itself was vibrant pink.

They stopped to watch a humming bird chase a blue jay. The jay flashed by squawking with its tiny enemy on its tail like a ruby bullet. The gaudy birds burst the colored air into a thousand glittering particles like metal confetti.

When they came out of this canyon, they saw below them a little green valley thick with trees, mostly eucalyptus, with here and there a poplar and one enormous black live-oak. Sliding and stumbling down a dry wash, they made for the valley.

Tod saw a man watching their approach from the edge of the wood. Faye also saw him and waved.

"Hi, Mig!" she shouted.

"Chinita!" he called back.

She ran the last ten yards of the slope and the man caught her in his arms.

He was toffee-colored with large Armenian eyes and pouting black lips. His head was a mass of tight, ordered curls. He wore a long-haired sweater, called a "gorilla" in and around Los Angeles, with nothing under it. His soiled duck trousers were held up by a red bandanna handkerchief. On his feet were a pair of tattered tennis sneakers.

They moved on to the camp which was located in a clearing in the center of the wood. It consisted of little more than a ramshackle hut patched with tin signs that had been stolen from the highway and a stove without legs or bottom set on some rocks. Near the hut was a row of chicken coops.

Earle started a fire under the stove while Faye sat down on a box and watched him. Tod went over to look at the chickens. There was one old hen and a half a dozen game cocks. A great deal of pains had been taken in making the coops, which were of grooved boards, carefully matched and joined. Their floors were freshly spread with peat moss.

The Mexican came over and began to talk about the cocks. He was very proud of them.

"That's Hermano, five times winner. He's one of Street's Butcher Boys. Pepe and El Negro are still stags. I fight them next week in San Pedro. That's Villa, he's a blinker, but still good. And that one's Zapata, twice winner, a Tassel Dom he is. And that's Jujutla. My champ."

He opened the coop and lifted the bird out for Tod.

"A murderer is what the guy is. Speedy and how!"

The cock's plumage was green, bronze and copper. Its beak was lemon and its legs orange.

"He's beautiful," Tod said.

"I'll say."

Mig tossed the bird back into the coop and they went back to join the others at the fire.

"When do we eat?" Faye asked.

Miguel tested the stove by spitting on it. He next found a large iron skillet and began to scour it with sand. Earle gave Faye a knife and some potatoes to peel, then picked up a burlap sack.

"I'll get the birds," he said.

Tod went along with him. They followed a narrow path

that looked as though it had been used by sheep until they came to a tiny field covered with high, tufted grass. Earle stopped behind a gum bush and held up his hand to warn Tod.

A mocking bird was singing near by. Its song was like pebbles being dropped one by one from a height into a pool of water. Then a quail began to call, using two soft guttural notes. Another quail answered and the birds talked back and forth. Their call was not like the cheerful whistle of the Eastern bobwhite. It was full of melancholy and weariness, yet marvelously sweet. Still another quail joined the duet. This one called from near the center of the field. It was a trapped bird, but the sound it made had no anxiety in it, only sadness, impersonal and without hope.

When Earle was satisfied that no one was there to spy on his poaching, he went to the trap. It was a wire basket about the size of a washtub with a small door in the top. He stooped over and began to fumble with the door. Five birds ran wildly along the inner edge and threw themselves at the wire. One of them, a cock, had a dainty plume on his head that curled forward almost to his beak.

Earle caught the birds one at a time and pulled their heads off before dropping them into his sack. Then he started back. As he walked along, he held the sack under his left arm. He lifted the birds out with his right hand and plucked them one at a time. Their feathers fell to the ground, point first, weighed down by the tiny drop of blood that trembled on the tips of their quills.

The sun went down before they reached the camp again. It grew chilly and Tod was glad of the fire. Faye shared her seat on the box with him and they both leaned forward into the heat.

Mig brought a jug of tequila from the hut. He filled a peanut butter jar for Faye and passed the jug to Tod.

The liquor smelled like rotten fruit, but he liked the taste. When he had had enough, Earle took it and then Miguel. They continued to pass it from hand to hand.

Earle tried to show Faye how plump the game was, but she wouldn't look. He gutted the birds, then began cutting them into quarters with a pair of heavy tin shears. Faye held her hands over her ears in order not to hear the soft click made by the blades as they cut through flesh and bone. Earle wiped the pieces with a rag and dropped them into the skillet where a large piece of lard was already sputtering.

For all her squeamishness, Faye ate as heartily as the men did. There was no coffee and they finished with tequila. They smoked and kept the jug moving. Faye tossed away the peanut butter jar and drank like the others, throwing her head back and tilting the jug.

Tod could sense her growing excitement. The box on which they were sitting was so small that their backs touched and he could feel how hot she was and how restless. Her neck and face had turned from ivory to rose. She kept reaching for his cigarettes.

Earle's features were hidden in the shadow of his big hat, but the Mexican sat full in the light of the fire. His skin glowed and the oil in his black curls sparkled. He kept smiling at Faye in a manner that Tod didn't like. The more he drank, the less he liked it.

Faye kept crowding Tod, so he left the box to sit on the ground where he could watch her better. She was smiling back at the Mexican. She seemed to know what he was thinking and to be thinking the same thing. Earle, too, became aware of what was passing between them. Tod heard him curse softly and saw him lean forward into the light and pick up a thick piece of firewood.

Mig laughed guiltily and began to sing.

"Las palmeras lloran por tu ausencia,
Las laguna se seco—ay!
La cerca de alambre que estaba en
El patio tambien se cayo!"

His voice was a plaintive tenor and it turned the revolutionary song into a sentimental lament, sweet and cloying. Faye joined in when he began another stanza. She didn't know the words, but she was able to carry the melody and to harmonize.

"Pues mi madre las cuidaba, ay!
Toditito se acabo—ay!"

Their voices touched in the thin, still air to form a minor chord and it was as though their bodies had touched. The song was transformed again. The melody remained the same, but the rhythm broke and its beat became ragged. It was a rumba now.

Earle shifted uneasily and played with his stick. Tod saw her look at him and saw that she was afraid, but instead of becoming wary, she grew still more reckless. She took a long pull at the jug and stood up. She put one hand on each of her buttocks and began to dance.

Mig seemed to have completely forgotten Earle. He clapped his hands, cupping them to make a hollow, drum-like sound, and put all he felt into his voice. He had changed to a more fitting song.

"Tony's wife,
The boys in Havana love Tony's wife . . ."

Faye had her hands clasped behind her head now and she rolled her hips to the broken beat. She was doing the "bump."

79

"Tony's wife,
They're fightin' their duels about Tony's
*   wife . . ."*

Perhaps Tod had been mistaken about Earle. He was
using his club on the back of the skillet, using it to bang
out the rhythm.

The Mexican stood up, still singing, and joined her in
the dance. They approached each other with short mincing
steps. She held her skirt up and out with her thumbs and
forefingers and he did the same with his trousers. They
met head on, blue-black against palegold, and used their
heads to pivot, then danced back to back with their buttocks touching, their knees bent and wide apart. While
Faye shook her breasts and her head, holding the rest of
her body rigid, he struck the soft ground heavily with his
feet and circled her. They faced each other again and
made believe they were cradling their behinds in a shawl.

Earle pounded the skillet harder and harder until it
rang like an anvil. Suddenly he, too, jumped up and
began to dance. He did a crude hoe-down. He leaped into
the air and knocked his heels together. He whooped. But
he couldn't become part of their dance. Its rhythm was like
a smooth glass wall between him and the dancers. No
matter how loudly he whooped or threw himself around, he
was unable to disturb the precision with which they retreated and advanced, separated and came together again.

Tod saw the blow before it fell. He saw Earle raise his
stick and bring it down on the Mexican's head. He heard
the crack and saw the Mexican go to his knees still dancing, his body unwilling or unable to acknowledge the in-
terruption.

Faye had her back to Mig when he fell, but she didn't
turn to look. She ran. She flashed by Tod. He reached

for her ankle to pull her down, but missed. He scrambled to his feet and ran after her.

If he caught her now, she wouldn't escape. He could hear her on the hill a little way ahead of him. He shouted to her, a deep, agonized bellow, like that a hound makes when it strikes a fresh line after hours of cold trailing. Already he could feel how it would be when he pulled her to the ground.

But the going was heavy and the stones and sand moved under his feet. He fell prone with his face in a clump of wild mustard that smelled of the rain and sun, clean, fresh and sharp. He rolled over on his back and stared up at the sky. The violent exercise had driven most of the heat out of his blood, but enough remained to make him tingle pleasantly. He felt comfortably relaxed, even happy.

Somewhere farther up the hill a bird began to sing. He listened. At first the low rich music sounded like water dripping on something hollow, the bottom of a silver pot perhaps, then like a stick dragged slowly over the strings of a harp. He lay quietly, listening.

When the bird grew silent, he made an effort to put Faye out of his mind and began to think about the series of cartoons he was making for his canvas of Los Angeles on fire. He was going to show the city burning at high noon, so that the flames would have to compete with the desert sun and thereby appear less fearful, more like bright flags flying from roofs and windows than a terrible holocaust. He wanted the city to have quite a gala air as it burned, to appear almost gay. And the people who set it on fire would be a holiday crowd.

The bird began to sing again. When it stopped, Faye was forgotten and he only wondered if he weren't exaggerating the importance of the people who come to California to die. Maybe they weren't really desperate enough to set a single city on fire, let alone the whole country. Maybe they were only the pick of America's madmen and not at all typical of the rest of the land.

He told himself that it didn't make any difference because he was an artist, not a prophet. His work would not be judged by the accuracy with which it foretold a future event but by its merit as painting. Nevertheless, he refused to give up the role of Jeremiah. He changed "pick of America's madmen" to "cream" and felt almost certain that the milk from which it had been skimmed was just as rich in violence. The Angelenos would be first, but their comrades all over the country would follow. There would be civil war.

He was amused by the strong feeling of satisfaction this dire conclusion gave him. Were all prophets of doom and destruction such happy men?

He stood up without trying to answer. When he reached the dirt road at the top of the canyon Faye and the car were gone.

15

"She went to the pictures with that Simpson guy," Harry told him when he called to see her the next night.

He sat down to wait for her. The old man was very ill and lay on the bed with extreme care as though it were a narrow shelf from which he might fall if he moved.

"What are they making on your lot?" he asked slowly, rolling his eyes toward Tod without budging his head.

" 'Manifest Destiny,' 'Sweet and Low Down,' 'Waterloo,' 'The Great Divide,' 'Begging Your . . .' "

" 'The Great Divide'—" Harry said, interrupting eagerly. "I remember that vehicle."

Tod realized he shouldn't have got him started, but there was nothing he could do about it now. He had to let him run down like a clock.

"When it opened I was playing the Irving in a little number called 'Enter Two Gents,' a trifle, but entertainment, real entertainment. I played a Jew comic, a Ben Welch effect, derby and big pants—'Pat, dey hoffered me a chob in de Heagle Laundreh' . . . 'Faith now, Ikey, and did you take it?' . . . 'No, who vants to vash heagles?' Joe Parvos played straight for me in a cop's suit. Well, the night 'The Great Divide' opened, Joe was laying up with a whisker in the old Fifth Avenue when the stove exploded. It was the broad's husband who blew the whistle. He was . . ."

He hadn't run down. He had stopped and was squeezing his left side with both hands.

Tod leaned over anxiously.

"Some water?"

Harry framed the word "no" with his lips, then groaned skillfully. It was a second-act curtain groan, so phony that Tod had to hide a smile. And yet, the old man's pallor hadn't come from a box.

Harry groaned again, modulating from pain to exhaustion, then closed his eyes. Tod saw how skillfully he got the maximum effect out of his agonized profile by using the pillow to set it off. He also noticed that Harry, like many actors, had very little back or top to his head. It was almost all face, like a mask, with deep furrows between the eyes, across the forehead and on either side of the nose and mouth, plowed there by years of broad grinning and heavy frowning. Because of them, he could never express anything either subtly or exactly. They wouldn't permit degrees of feeling, only the furthest degree.

Tod began to wonder if it might not be true that actors suffer less than other people. He thought about this for a while, then decided that he was wrong. Feeling is of the heart and nerves and the crudeness of its expression has nothing to do with its intensity. Harry suffered as keenly as anyone, despite the theatricality of his groans and grimaces.

He seemed to enjoy suffering. But not all kinds, certainly not sickness. Like many people, he only enjoyed the sort that was self-inflicted. His favorite method was to bare his soul to strangers in barrooms. He would make believe he was drunk, and stumble over to where some strangers were sitting. He usually began by reciting a poem.

"Let me sit down for a moment,
I have a stone in my shoe.
I was once blithe and happy,
I was once young like you."

If his audience shouted, "scram, bum!" he only smiled humbly and went on with his act.

"Have pity, folks, on my gray hair . . ."

The bartender or someone else had to stop him by force, otherwise he would go on no matter what was said to him. Once he got started everyone in the bar usually listened, for he gave a great performance. He roared and whispered, commanded and cajoled. He imitated the whimper of a little girl crying for her vanished mother, as well as the different dialects of the many cruel managers he had known. He even did the off-stage noises, twittering like birds to herald the dawn of Love and yelping like a pack of bloodhounds when describing how an Evil Fate ever pursued him.

He made his audience see him start out in his youth to play Shakespeare in the auditorium of the Cambridge Latin School, full of glorious dreams, burning with ambition. Follow him, as still a mere stripling, he starved in a Broadway rooming house, an idealist who desired only to share his art with the world. Stand with him, as, in the prime of manhood, he married a beautiful dancer, a headliner on the Gus Sun time. Be close behind him as, one night, he returned home unexpectedly to find her in the arms of a head usher. Forgive, as he forgave, out of the goodness of his heart and the greatness of his love. Then laugh, tasting the bitter gall, when the very next night he found her in the arms of a booking agent. Again he forgave her and again she sinned. Even then he didn't cast her out, no, though she jeered, mocked and even struck him repeatedly with an umbrella. But she ran off with a foreigner, a swarthy magician fellow. Behind she left memories and their baby daughter. He made his audience shadow him still as misfortune followed misfortune and, a middle-aged man, he haunted the booking offices, only a ghost of his former self. He who had hoped to play Hamlet, Lear, Othello, must needs become the Co. in an act called Nat Plumstone & Co., light quips and breezy patter. He made them dog his dragging feet as, an aged and trembling old man, he . . .

Faye came in quietly. Tod started to greet her, but she put her finger to her lips for him to be silent and motioned toward the bed.

The old man was asleep. Tod thought his worn, dry skin looked like eroded ground. The few beads of sweat that glistened on his forehead and temples carried no promise of relief. It might rot, like rain that comes too late to a field, but could never refresh.

They both tiptoed out of the room.

In the hall he asked if she had had a good time with Homer.

"That dope!" she exclaimed, making a wry face. "He's strictly home-cooking."

Tod started to ask some more questions, but she dismissed him with a curt, "I'm tired, honey."

16

The next afternoon, Tod was on his way upstairs when he saw a crowd in front of the door to the Greeners' apartment. They were excited and talked in whispers.

"What's happened?" he asked.

"Harry's dead."

He tried the door of the apartment. It wasn't locked, so he went in. The corpse lay stretched out on the bed, completely covered with a blanket. From Faye's room came the sound of crying. He knocked softly on her door. She opened it for him, then turned without saying a word, and stumbled to her bed. She was sobbing into a face towel.

He stood in the doorway, without knowing what to do or say. Finally, he went over to the bed and tried to comfort her. He patted her shoulder.

"You poor kid."

She was wearing a tattered, black lace negligee that had large rents in it. When he leaned over her, he noticed that her skin gave off a warm, sweet odor, like that of buckwheat in flower.

He turned away and lit a cigarette. There was a knock on the door. When he opened it, Mary Dove rushed past him to take Faye in her arms.

Mary also told Faye to be brave. She phrased it differently than he had done, however, and made it sound a lot more convincing.

"Show some guts, kid. Come on now, show some guts."

Faye shoved her away and stood up. She took a few wild steps, then sat down on the bed again.

"I killed him," she groaned.

Mary and he both denied this emphatically.

"I killed him, I tell you! I did! I did!"

She began to call herself names. Mary wanted to stop her, but Tod told her not to. Faye had begun to act and he felt that if they didn't interfere she would manage an escape for herself.

"She'll talk herself quiet," he said.

In a voice heavy with self-accusation, she began to tell what had happened. She had come home from the studio and found Harry in bed. She asked him how he was, but didn't wait for an answer. Instead, she turned her back on him to examine herself in the wall mirror. While fixing her face, she told him that she had seen Ben Murphy and that Ben had said if Harry were feeling better he might be able to use him in a Bowery sequence. She had been surprised when he didn't shout as he always did when Ben's name was mentioned. He was jealous of Ben and always shouted, "To hell with that bastard; I knew him when he cleaned spittoons in a nigger barroom."

She realized that he must be pretty sick. She didn't turn around because she noticed what looked like the beginning of a pimple. It was only a speck of dirt and she wiped it off, but then she had to do her face all over again. While she was working at it, she told him that she could get a job as a dress extra if she had a new evening gown. Just to kid him, she looked tough and said, "If you can't buy me an evening gown, I'll find someone who can."

When he didn't say anything, she got sore and began to sing, "Jeepers Creepers." He didn't tell her to shut up, so she knew something must be wrong. She ran over to the couch. He was dead.

As soon as she had finished telling all this, she began to sob in a lower key, almost a coo, and rocked herself back and forth.

"Poor papa . . . Poor darling . . ."

The fun they used to have together when she was little. No matter how hard up he was, he always bought her dolls and candy, and no matter how tired, he always played with her. She used to ride piggy-back and they would roll on the floor and laugh and laugh.

Mary's sobs made Faye speed up her own and they both began to get out of hand.

There was a knock on the door. Tod answered it and found Mrs. Johnson, the janitress. Faye shook her head for him not to let her in.

"Come back later," Tod said.

He shut the door in her face. A minute later it opened again and Mrs. Johnson entered boldly. She had used a pass-key.

"Get out," he said.

She tried to push past him, but he held her until Faye told him to let her go.

He disliked Mrs. Johnson intensely. She was an officious, bustling woman with a face like a baked apple, soft and blotched. Later he found out that her hobby was funerals. Her preoccupation with them wasn't morbid; it was formal. She was interested in the arrangement of the flowers, the order of the procession, the clothing and deportment of the mourners.

She went straight to Faye and stopped her sobs with a firm, "Now, Miss Greener."

There was so much authority in her voice and manner that she succeeded where Mary and Tod had failed.

Faye looked up at her respectfully.

"First, my dear," Mrs. Johnson said, counting one with the thumb of her right hand on the index finger of her left, "first, I want you to understand that my sole desire in this matter is to help you."

She looked hard at Mary, then at Tod.

"I don't get anything out of it, and it's just a lot of trouble."

"Yes," Faye said.

"All right. There are several things I have to know, if I'm to help you. Did the deceased leave any money or insurance?"

"No."

"Have you any money?"

"No."

"Can you borrow any?"

"I don't think so."

Mrs. Johnson sighed.

"Then the city will have to bury him."

Faye didn't comment.

"Don't you understand, child, the city will have to bury him in a pauper's grave?"

She put so much contempt into "city" and horror into "pauper" that Faye flushed and began to sob again.

Mrs. Johnson made as though to walk out, even took several steps in the direction of the door, then changed her mind and came back.

"How much does a funeral cost?" Faye asked.

"Two hundred dollars. But you can pay on the installment plan—fifty dollars down and twenty-five a month."

Mary and Tod both spoke together.

"I'll get the money."

"I've got some."

"That's fine," Mrs. Johnson said. "You'll need at least fifty more for incidental expenses. I'll go ahead and take care of everything. Mr. Holsepp will bury your father. He'll do it right."

She shook hands with Faye, as though she were congratulating her, and hurried out of the room.

Mrs. Johnson's little business talk had apparently done Faye some good. Her lips were set and her eyes dry.

"Don't worry," Tod said. "I can raise the money."

"No, thanks," she said.

Mary opened her purse and took out a roll of bills.

"Here's some."

"No," she said, pushing it away.

She sat thinking for a while, then went to the dressing table and began to fix her tear-stained face. She wore a hard smile as she worked. Suddenly she turned, lipstick in air, and spoke to Mary.

"Can you get me into Mrs. Jenning's?"

"What for?" Tod demanded. "I'll get the money."

Both girls ignored him.

"Sure," said Mary, "you ought to done that long ago. It's a soft touch."

Faye laughed.

"I was saving it."

The change that had come over both of them startled Tod. They had suddenly become very tough.

"For a punkola like that Earle. Get smart, girlie, and lay off the cheapies. Let him ride a horse, he's a cowboy, ain't he?"

They laughed shrilly and went into the bathroom with their arms around each other.

Tod thought he understood their sudden change to slang. It made them feel worldly and realistic, and so more able to cope with serious things.

He knocked on the bathroom door.

"What do *you* want?" Faye called out.

"Listen, kid," he said, trying to imitate them. "Why go on the turf? I can get the dough."

"Oh, yeah! No, thanks," Faye said.

"But listen . . ." he began again.

"Go peddle your tripe!" Mary shouted.

17

On the day of Harry's funeral Tod was drunk. He hadn't seen Faye since she went off with Mary Dove, but he knew that he was certain to find her at the undertaking parlor and he wanted to have the courage to quarrel with her. He started drinking at lunch. When he got to Holsepp's in the late afternoon, he had passed the brave state and was well into the ugly one.

He found Harry in his box, waiting to be wheeled out for exhibition in the adjoining chapel. The casket was open and the old man looked quite snug. Drawn up to a little below his shoulders and folded back to show its fancy lining was an ivory satin coverlet. Under his head was a tiny lace cushion. He was wearing a Tuxedo, or at least had on a black bow tie with his stiff shirt and wing collar. His face had been newly shaved, his eyebrows shaped and plucked and his lips and cheeks rouged. He looked like the interlocutor in a minstrel show.

Tod bowed his head as though in silent prayer when he heard someone come in. He recognized Mrs. Johnson's voice and turned carefully to face her. He caught her eye and nodded, but she ignored him. She was busy with a man in a badly fitting frock coat.

"It's the principle of the thing," she scolded. "Your estimate said bronze. Those handles ain't bronze and you know it."

"But I asked Miss Greener," whined the man. "She okayed them."

"I don't care. I'm surprised at you, trying to save a few dollars by fobbing off a set of cheap gun-metal handles on the poor child."

Tod didn't wait for the undertaker to answer. He had seen Faye pass the door on the arm of one of the Lee sisters. When he caught up with her, he didn't know what to say. She misunderstood his agitation and was touched. She sobbed a little for him.

She had never looked more beautiful. She was wearing a new, very tight black dress and her platinum hair was tucked up in a shining bun under a black straw sailor. Ever so often, she carried a tiny lace handkerchief to her eyes and made it flutter there for a moment. But all he could think of was that she had earned the money for her outfit on her back.

She grew uneasy under his stare and started to edge away. He caught her arm.

"May I speak with you for a minute, alone?"

Miss Lee took the hint and left.

"What is it?" Faye asked.

"Not here," he whispered, making mystery out of his uncertainty.

He led her along the hall until he found an empty showroom. On the walls were framed photographs of important funerals and on little stands and tables were samples of coffin materials, and models of tombstones and mausoleums.

Not knowing what to say, he accented his awkwardness, playing the inoffensive fool.

She smiled and became almost friendly.

"Give out, you big dope."

"A kiss . . ."

"Sure, baby," she laughed, "only don't muss me." They pecked at each other.

She tried to get away, but he held her. She became annoyed and demanded an explanation. He searched his head for one. It wasn't his head he should have searched, however.

She was leaning toward him, drooping slightly, but not from fatigue. He had seen young birches droop like that at midday when they are over-heavy with sun.

"You're drunk," she said, pushing him away.

"Please," he begged.

"Le'go, you bastard."

Raging at him, she was still beautiful. That was because her beauty was structural like a tree's, not a quality of her mind or heart. Perhaps even whoring couldn't damage it for that reason, only age or accident or disease.

In a minute she would scream for help. He had to say something. She wouldn't understand the aesthetic argument and with what values could he back up the moral one? The economic didn't make sense either. Whoring certainly paid. Half of the customer's thirty dollars. Say ten men a week.

She kicked at his shins, but he held on to her. Suddenly he began to talk. He had found an argument. Disease would destroy her beauty. He shouted at her like a Y.M.C.A. lecturer on sex hygiene.

She stopped struggling and held her head down, sobbing fitfully. When he was through, he let go of her arms and she bolted from the room. He groped his way to a carved, marble coffin.

He was still sitting there when a young man in a black jacket and gray striped trousers came in.

"Are you here for the Greener funeral?"

Tod stood up and nodded vaguely.

"The services are beginning," the man said, then opened a little casket covered with grosgrain satin and took out a dust cloth. Tod watched him go around the showroom wiping off the samples.

"Services have probably started," the man repeated with a wave at the door.

Tod understood this time and left. The only exit he could find led through the chapel. The moment he entered it, Mrs. Johnson caught him and directed him to a seat.

He wanted badly to get away, but it was impossible to do so without making a scene.

Faye was sitting in the front row of benches, facing the pulpit. She had the Lee sisters on one side and Mary Dove and Abe Kusich on the other. Behind them sat the tenants of the San Berdoo, occupying about six rows. Tod was alone in the seventh. After him were several empty rows and then a scattering of men and women who looked very much out of place.

He turned in order not to see Faye's jerking shoulders and examined the people in the last rows. He knew their kind. While not torch-bearers themselves, they would run behind the fire and do a great deal of the shouting. They had come to see Harry buried, hoping for a dramatic incident of some sort, hoping at least for one of the mourners to be led weeping hysterically from the chapel. It seemed to Tod that they stared back at him with an expression of vicious, acrid boredom that trembled on the edge of violence. When they began to mutter among themselves, he half-turned and watched them out of the corner of his eyes.

An old woman with a face pulled out of shape by badly-fitting store teeth came in and whispered to a man sucking on the handle of a home-made walking stick. He passed her message along and they all stood up and went out hurriedly. Tod guessed that some star had been seen going into a restaurant by one of their scouts. If so, they would wait outside the place for hours until the star came out again or the police drove them away.

The Gingo family arrived soon after they had left. The Gingos were Eskimos who had been brought to Hollywood to make retakes for a picture about polar exploration. Although it had been released long ago, they refused to return to Alaska. They liked Hollywood.

Harry had been a good friend of theirs and had eaten

with them quite regularly, sharing the smoked salmon, white fish, marinated and maatjes herrings they bought at Jewish delicatessen stores. He also shared the great quantities of cheap brandy they mixed with hot water and salt butter and drank out of tin cups.

Mama and Papa Gingo, trailed by their son, moved down the center aisle of the chapel, bowing and waving to everyone, until they reached the front row. Here they gathered around Faye and shook hands with her, each one in turn. Mrs. Johnson tried to make them go to one of the back rows, but they ignored her orders and sat down in front.

The overhead lights of the chapel were suddenly dimmed. Simultaneously other lights went on behind imitation stained-glass windows which hung on the fake oak-paneled walls. There was a moment of hushed silence, broken only by Faye's sobs, then an electric organ started to play a recording of one of Bach's chorales, "Come Redeemer, Our Saviour."

Tod recognized the music. His mother often played a piano adaptation of it on Sundays at home. It very politely asked Christ to come, in clear and honest tones with just the proper amount of supplication. The God it invited was not the King of Kings, but a shy and gentle Christ, a maiden surrounded by maidens, and the invitation was to a lawn fete, not to the home of some weary, suffering sinner. It didn't plead; it urged with infinite grace and delicacy, almost as though it were afraid of frightening the prospective guest.

So far as Tod could tell, no one was listening to the music. Faye was sobbing and the others seemed busy inside themselves. Bach politely serenading Christ was not for them.

The music would soon change its tone and grow exciting. He wondered if that would make any difference. Already the bass was beginning to throb. He noticed that it made the Eskimos uneasy. As the bass gained in power and began to dominate the treble, he heard Papa Gingo grunt with pleasure. Mama caught Mrs. Johnson eyeing him, and put her fat hand on the back of his head to keep him quiet.

"Now come, O our Saviour," the music begged. Gone was its diffidence and no longer was it polite. Its struggle with the bass had changed it. Even a hint of a threat crept in and a little impatience. Of doubt, however, he could not detect the slightest trace.

If there was a hint of a threat, he thought, just a hint, and a tiny bit of impatience, could Bach be blamed? After all, when he wrote this music, the world had already been waiting for its lover more than seventeen hundred years. But the music changed again and both threat and impatience disappeared. The treble soared free and triumphant and the bass no longer struggled to keep it down. It had become a rich accompaniment. "Come or don't come," the music seemed to say, "I love you and my love is enough." It was a simple statement of fact, neither cry nor serenade, made without arrogance or humility.

Perhaps Christ heard. If He did, He gave no sign. The attendants heard, for it was their cue to trundle on Harry in his box. Mrs. Johnson followed close behind and saw to it that the casket was properly placed. She raised her hand and Bach was silenced in the middle of a phrase.

"Will those of you who wish to view the deceased before the sermon please step forward?" she called out.

Only the Gingos stood up immediately. They made for the coffin in a group. Mrs. Johnson held them back and motioned for Faye to look first. Supported by Mary Dove and the Lee girls, she took a quick peek, increased the tempo of her sobs for a moment, then hurried back to the bench.

The Gingos had their chance next. They leaned over the coffin and told each other something in a series of thick, explosive gutturals. When they tried to take another look, Mrs. Johnson herded them firmly to their seats.

The dwarf sidled up to the box, made a play with his handkerchief and retreated. When no one followed him, Mrs. Johnson lost patience, seeming to take what she understood as a lack of interest for a personal insult.

"Those who wish to view the remains of the late Mr. Greener must do so at once," she barked.

There was a little stir, but no one stood up.

"You, Mrs. Gail," she finally said, looking directly at the person named. "How about you? Don't you want a last look? Soon all that remains of your neighbor will be buried forever."

There was no getting out of it. Mrs. Gail moved down the aisle, trailed by several others.

Tod used them to cover his escape.

18

Faye moved out of the San Berdoo the day after the funeral. Tod didn't know where she had gone and was getting up the courage to call Mrs. Jenning when he saw her from the window of his office. She was dressed in the costume of a Napoleonic vivandière. By the time he got the window open, she had almost turned the corner of the building. He shouted for her to wait. She waved, but when he got downstairs she was gone.

From her dress, he was sure that she was working in the picture called "Waterloo." He asked a studio policeman where the company was shooting and was told on the back lot. He started toward it at once. A platoon of cuirassiers, big men mounted on gigantic horses, went by. He knew that they must be headed for the same set and followed them. They broke into a gallop and he was soon outdistanced.

The sun was very hot. His eyes and throat were choked with the dust thrown up by the horses' hooves and his head throbbed. The only bit of shade he could find was under an ocean liner made of painted canvas with real lifeboats hanging from its davits. He stood in its narrow shadow for a while, then went on toward a great forty-foot papier mâché sphinx that loomed up in the distance. He had to cross a desert to reach it, a desert that was continually being made larger by a fleet of trucks dumping white sand. He had gone only a few feet when a man with a megaphone ordered him off.

He skirted the desert, making a wide turn to the right, and came to a Western street with a plank sidewalk. On the porch of the "Last Chance Saloon" was a rocking chair. He sat down on it and lit a cigarette.

From there he could see a jungle compound with a water buffalo tethered to the side of a conical grass hut. Every few seconds the animal groaned musically. Suddenly an Arab charged by on a white stallion. He shouted at the man, but got no answer. A little while later he saw a truck with a load of snow and several malamute dogs. He shouted again. The driver shouted something back, but didn't stop.

Throwing away his cigarette, he went through the swinging doors of the saloon. There was no back to the building and he found himself in a Paris street. He followed it to its end, coming out in a Romanesque courtyard. He heard voices a short distance away and went toward them. On a lawn of fiber, a group of men and women in riding costume were picnicking. They were eating cardboard food in front of a cellophane waterfall. He started toward them to ask his way, but was stopped by a man who scowled and held up a sign—"Quiet, Please, We're Shooting."

When Tod took another step forward, the man shook his fist threateningly.

Next he came to a small pond with large celluloid swans floating on it. Across one end was a bridge with a sign that read, "To Kamp Komfit." He crossed the bridge and followed a little path that ended at a Greek temple dedicated to Eros. The god himself lay face downward in a pile of old newspapers and bottles.

From the steps of the temple, he could see in the distance a road lined with Lombardy poplars. It was the one on which he had lost the cuirassiers. He pushed his way through a tangle of briars, old flats and iron junk, skirting the skeleton of a Zeppelin, a bamboo stockade, an adobe fort, the wooden horse of Troy, a flight of baroque palace stairs that started in a bed of weeds and ended against the branches of an oak, part of the Fourteenth Street elevated station, a Dutch windmill, the bones of a dinosaur, the upper half of the Merrimac, a corner of a Mayan temple, until he finally reached the road.

He was out of breath. He sat down under one of the poplars on a rock made of brown plaster and took off his jacket. There was a cool breeze blowing and he soon felt more comfortable.

He had lately begun to think not only of Goya and Daumier but also of certain Italian artists of the seventeenth and eighteenth centuries, of Salvator Rosa, Francesco Guardi and Monsu Desiderio, the painters of Decay and Mystery. Looking downhill now, he could see compositions that might have actually been arranged from the Calabrian work of Rosa. There were partially demolished buildings and broken monuments, half-hidden by great, tortured trees, whose exposed roots writhed dramatically in the arid ground, and by shrubs that carried, not flowers or berries, but armories of spikes, hooks and swords.

For Guardi and Desiderio there were bridges which

bridged nothing, sculpture in trees, palaces that seemed of marble until a whole stone portico began to flap in the light breeze. And there were figures as well. A hundred yards from where Tod was sitting a man in a derby hat leaned drowsily against the gilded poop of a Venetian barque and peeled an apple. Still farther on, a charwoman on a stepladder was scrubbing with soap and water the face of a Buddha thirty feet high.

He left the road and climbed across the spine of the hill to look down on the other side. From there he could see a ten-acre field of cockleburs spotted with clumps of sunflowers and wild gum. In the center of the field was a gigantic pile of sets, flats and props. While he watched, a ten-ton truck added another load to it. This was the final dumping ground. He thought of Janvier's "Sargasso Sea." Just as that imaginary body of water was a history of civilization in the form of a marine junkyard, the studio lot was one in the form of a dream dump. A Sargasso of the imagination! And the dump grew continually, for there wasn't a dream afloat somewhere which wouldn't sooner or later turn up on it, having first been made photographic by plaster, canvas, lath and paint. Many boats sink and never reach the Sargasso, but no dream ever entirely disappears. Somewhere it troubles some unfortunate person and some day, when that person has been sufficiently troubled, it will be reproduced on the lot.

When he saw a red glare in the sky and heard the rumble of cannon, he knew it must be Waterloo. From around a bend in the road trotted several cavalry regiments. They wore casques and chest armor of black cardboard and carried long horse pistols in their saddle holsters. They were Victor Hugo's soldiers. He had worked on some of the drawings for their uniforms himself, following carefully the descriptions in "Les Miserables."

He went in the direction they took. Before long he was

passed by the men of Lefebvre-Desnouttes, followed by a regiment of gendarmes d'élite, several companies of chasseurs of the guard and a flying detachment of Rimbaud's lancers.

They must be moving up for the disastrous attack on La Haite Santée. He hadn't read the scenario and wondered if it had rained yesterday. Would Grouchy or Bulcher arrive? Grotenstein, the producer, might have changed it.

The sound of cannon was becoming louder all the time and the red fan in the sky more intense. He could smell the sweet, pungent odor of blank powder. It might be over before he could get there. He started to run. When he topped a rise after a sharp bend in the road, he found a great plain below him covered with early nineteenth-century troops, wearing all the gay and elaborate uniforms that used to please him so much when he was a child and spent long hours looking at the soldiers in an old dictionary. At the far end of the field, he could see an enormous hump around which the English and their allies were gathered. It was Mont St. Jean and they were getting ready to defend it gallantly. It wasn't quite finished, however, and swarmed with grips, property men, set dressers, carpenters and painters.

Tod stood near a eucalyptus tree to watch, concealing himself behind a sign that read, " 'Waterloo'—A Charles H. Grotenstein Production." Nearby a youth in a carefully torn horse guard's uniform was being rehearsed in his lines by one of the assistant directors.

"Vive l'Empereur!" the young man shouted, then clutched his breast and fell forward dead. The assistant director was a hard man to please and made him do it over and over again.

In the center of the plain, the battle was going ahead briskly. Things looked tough for the British and their allies.

The Prince of Orange commanding the center, Hill the right and Picton the left wing, were being pressed hard by the veteran French. The desperate and intrepid Prince was in an especially bad spot. Tod heard him cry hoarsely above the din of battle, shouting to the Hollande-Belgians, "Nassau! Brunswick! Never retreat!" Nevertheless, the retreat began. Hill, too, fell back. The French killed General Picton with a ball through the head and he returned to his dressing room. Alten was put to the sword and also retired. The colors of the Lunenberg battalion, borne by a prince of the family of Deux-Ponts, were captured by a famous child star in the uniform of a Parisian drummer boy. The Scotch Greys were destroyed and went to change into another uniform. Ponsonby's heavy dragoons were also cut to ribbons. Mr. Grotenstein would have a large bill to pay at the Western Costume Company.

Neither Napoleon nor Wellington was to be seen. In Wellington's absence, one of the assistant directors, a Mr. Crane, was in command of the allies. He reinforced his center with one of Chasse's brigades and one of Wincke's. He supported these with infantry from Brunswick, Welsh foot, Devon yeomanry and Hanoverian light horse with oblong leather caps and flowing plumes of horsehair.

For the French, a man in a checked cap ordered Milhaud's cuirassiers to carry Mont St. Jean. With their sabers in their teeth and their pistols in their hands, they charged. It was a fearful sight.

The man in the checked cap was making a fatal error. Mont St. Jean was unfinished. The paint was not yet dry and all the struts were not in place. Because of the thickness of the cannon smoke, he had failed to see that the hill was still being worked on by property men, grips and carpenters.

It was the classic mistake, Tod realized, the same one Napoleon had made. Then it had been wrong for a different reason. The Emperor had ordered the cuirassiers to charge Mont St. Jean not knowing that a deep ditch was hidden at its foot to trap his heavy cavalry. The result had been disaster for the French; the beginning of the end.

This time the same mistake had a different outcome. Waterloo, instead of being the end of the Grand Army, resulted in a draw. Neither side won, and it would have to be fought over again the next day. Big losses, however, were sustained by the insurance company in workmen's compensation. The man in the checked cap was sent to the dog house by Mr. Grotenstein just as Napoleon was sent to St. Helena.

When the front rank of Milhaud's heavy division started up the slope of Mont St. Jean, the hill collapsed. The noise was terrific. Nails screamed with agony as they pulled out of joists. The sound of ripping canvas was like that of little children whimpering. Lath and scantling snapped as though they were brittle bones. The whole hill folded like an enormous umbrella and covered Napoleon's army with painted cloth.

It turned into a route. The victors of Bersina, Leipsic, Austerlitz, fled like schoolboys who had broken a pane of glass. "Sauve qui peut!" they cried, or, rather, "Scram!"

The armies of England and her allies were too deep in scenery to flee. They had to wait for the carpenters and ambulances to come up. The men of the gallant Seventy-Fifth Highlanders were lifted out of the wreck with block and tackle. They were carted off by the stretcher-bearers, still clinging bravely to their claymores.

19

Tod got a lift back to his office in a studio car. He had to ride on the running board because the seats were occupied by two Walloon grenadiers and four Swabian foot. One of the infantrymen had a broken leg, the other extras were only scratched and bruised. They were quite happy about their wounds. They were certain to receive several extra days' pay, and the man with the broken leg thought he might get as much as five hundred dollars.

When Tod arrived at his office, he found Faye waiting to see him. She hadn't been in the battle. At the last moment, the director had decided not to use any vivandières.

To his surprise, she greeted him with warm friendliness. Nevertheless, he tried to apologize for his behavior in the funeral parlor. He had hardly started before she interrupted him. She wasn't angry, but grateful for his lecture on venereal disease. It had brought her to her senses.

She had still another surprise for him. She was living in Homer Simpson's house. The arrangement was a business one. Homer had agreed to board and dress her until she became a star. They were keeping a record of every cent he spent and as soon as she clicked in pictures, she would pay him back with six per cent interest. To make it absolutely legal, they were going to have a lawyer draw up a contract.

She pressed Tod for an opinion and he said it was a splendid idea. She thanked him and invited him to dinner for the next night.

After she had gone, he wondered what living with her would do to Homer. He thought it might straighten him out. He fooled himself into believing this with an image, as though a man were a piece of iron to be heated and then straightened with hammer blows. He should have known better, for if anyone ever lacked malleability Homer did.

He continued to make this mistake when he had dinner with them. Faye seemed very happy, talking about charge accounts and stupid sales clerks. Homer had a flower in his buttonhole, wore carpet slippers and beamed at her continually.

After they had eaten, while Homer was in the kitchen washing dishes, Tod got her to tell him what they did with themselves all day. She said that they lived quietly and that she was glad because she was tired of excitement. All she wanted was a career. Homer did the housework and she was getting a real rest. Daddy's long sickness had tired her out completely. Homer liked to do housework and anyway he wouldn't let her go into the kitchen because of her hands.

"Protecting his investment," Tod said.

"Yes," she replied seriously, "they have to be beautiful."

They had breakfast around ten, she went on. Homer brought it to her in bed. He took a housekeeping magazine and fixed the tray like the pictures in it. While she bathed and dressed, he cleaned the house. Then they went downtown to the stores and she bought all sorts of things, mostly clothes. They didn't eat lunch on account of her figure, but usually had dinner out and went to the movies.

"Then, ice cream sodas," Homer finished for her, as he came out of the kitchen.

Faye laughed and excused herself. They were going to a picture and she wanted to change her dress. When she had left, Homer suggested that they get some air in the patio. He made Tod take the deck chair while he sat on an upturned orange crate.

If he had been careful and had acted decently, Tod couldn't help thinking, she might be living with him. He was at least better looking than Homer. But then there was her other prerequisite. Homer had an income and lived in a house, while he earned thirty dollars a week and lived in a furnished room.

The happy grin on Homer's face made him feel ashamed

of himself. He was being unfair. Homer was a humble, grateful man who would never laugh at her, who was incapable of laughing at anything. Because of this great quality, she could live with him on what she considered a much higher plane.

"What's the matter?" Homer asked softly, laying one of his heavy hands on Tod's knee.

"Nothing. Why?"

Tod moved so that the hand slipped off.

"You were making faces."

"I was thinking of something."

"Oh," Homer said sympathetically.

Tod couldn't resist asking an ugly question.

"When are you two getting married?"

Homer looked hurt.

"Didn't Faye tell about us?"

"Yes, sort of."

"It's a business arrangement."

"Yes?"

To make Tod believe it, he poured out a long, disjointed argument, the one he must have used on himself. He even went further than the business part and claimed that they were doing it for poor Harry's sake. Faye had nothing left in the world except her career and she must succeed for her daddy's sake. The reason she wasn't a star was because she didn't have the right clothes. He had money and believed in her talent, so it was only natural for them to enter into a business arrangement. Did Tod know a good lawyer?

It was a rhetorical question, but would become a real one, painfully insistent, if Tod smiled. He frowned. That was wrong, too.

"We must see a lawyer this week and have papers drawn up."

His eagerness was pathetic. Tod wanted to help him,

but didn't know what to say. He was still fumbling for an answer when they heard a woman shouting from the hill behind the garage.

"Adore! Adore!"

She had a high soprano voice, very clear and pure.

"What a funny name," Tod said, glad to change the subject.

"Maybe it's a foreigner," Homer said.

The woman came into the yard from around the corner of the garage. She was eager and plump and very American.

"Have you seen my little boy?" she asked, making a gesture of helplessness. "Adore's such a wanderer."

Homer surprised Tod by standing up and smiling at the woman. Faye had certainly helped his timidity.

"Is your son lost?" Homer said.

"Oh, no—just hiding to tease me."

She held out her hand.

"We're neighbors. I'm Maybelle Loomis."

"Glad to know you, ma'am. I'm Homer Simpson and this is Mr. Hackett."

Tod also shook hands with her.

"Have you been living here long?" she asked.

"No. I've just come from the East," Homer said.

"Oh, have you? I've been here ever since Mr. Loomis passed on six years ago. I'm an old settler."

"You like it then?" Tod asked.

"Like California?" she laughed at the idea that anyone might not like it. "Why, it's a paradise on earth!"

"Yes," Homer agreed gravely.

"And anyway," she went on, "I have to live here on account of Adore."

"Is he sick?"

"Oh, no. On account of his career. His agent calls him the biggest little attraction in Hollywood."

She spoke so vehemently that Homer flinched.

"He's in the movies?" Tod asked.

"I'll say," she snapped.

Homer tried to placate her.

"That's very nice."

"If it weren't for favoritism," she said bitterly, "he'd be a star. It ain't talent. It's pull. What's Shirley Temple got that he ain't got?"

"Why, I don't know," Homer mumbled.

She ignored this and let out a fearful bellow.

"Adore! Adore!"

Tod had seen her kind around the studio. She was one of that army of women who drag their children from casting office to casting office and sit for hours, weeks, months, waiting for a chance to show what Junior can do. Some of them are very poor, but no matter how poor, they always manage to scrape together enough money, often by making great sacrifices, to send their children to one of the innumerable talent schools.

"Adore!" she yelled once more, then laughed and became a friendly housewife again, a chubby little person with dimples in her fat cheeks and fat elbows.

"Have you any children, Mr. Simpson?" she asked.

"No," he replied, blushing.

"You're lucky—they're a nuisance."

She laughed to show that she didn't really mean it and called her child again.

"Adore . . . Oh, Adore . . ."

Her next question surprised them both.

"Who do you follow?"

"What?" said Tod.

"I mean—in the Search for Health, along the Road of Life?"

They both gaped at her.

"I'm a raw-foodist, myself," she said. "Dr. Pierce is our

leader. You must have seen his ads—'Know-All Pierce-All.'"

"Oh, yes," Tod said, "you're vegetarians."

She laughed at his ignorance.

"Far from it. We're much stricter. Vegetarians eat cooked vegetables. We eat only raw ones. Death comes from eating dead things."

Neither Tod nor Homer found anything to say.

"Adore," she began again. "Adore . . ."

This time there was an answer from around the corner of the garage.

"Here I am, mama."

A minute later, a little boy appeared dragging behind him a small sailboat on wheels. He was about eight years old, with a pale, peaked face and a large, troubled forehead. He had great staring eyes. His eyebrows had been plucked and shaped carefully. Except for his Buster Brown collar, he was dressed like a man, in long trousers, vest and jacket.

He tried to kiss his mother, but she fended him off and pulled at his clothes, straightening and arranging them with savage little tugs.

"Adore," she said sternly, "I want you to meet Mr. Simpson, our neighbor."

Turning like a soldier at the command of a drill sergeant, he walked up to Homer and grasped his hand.

"A pleasure, sir," he said, bowing stiffly with his heels together.

"That's the way they do it in Europe," Mrs. Loomis beamed. "Isn't he cute?"

"What a pretty sailboat!" Homer said, trying to be friendly.

Both mother and son ignored his comment. She pointed to Tod, and the child repeated his bow and heel-click.

"Well, we've got to go," she said.

Tod watched the child, who was standing a little to one side of his mother and making faces at Homer. He rolled his eyes back in his head so that only the whites showed and twisted his lips in a snarl.

Mrs. Loomis noticed Tod's glance and turned sharply. When she saw what Adore was doing, she yanked him by the arm, jerking him clear off the ground.

"Adore!" she yelled.

To Tod she said apologetically, "He thinks he's the Frankenstein monster."

She picked the boy up, hugging and kissing him ardently. Then she set him down again and fixed his rumpled clothing.

"Won't Adore sing something for us?" Tod asked.

"No," the little boy said sharply.

"Adore," his mother scolded, "sing at once."

"That's all right, if he doesn't feel like it," Homer said.

But Mrs. Loomis was determined to have him sing. She could never permit him to refuse an audience.

"Sing, Adore," she repeated with quiet menace. "Sing 'Mama Doan Wan' No Peas.'"

His shoulders twitched as though they already felt the strap. He tilted his straw sailor over one eye, buttoned up his jacket and did a little strut, then began:

"Mama doan wan' no peas,
An' rice, an' cocoanut oil,
Just a bottle of brandy handy all the day.
Mama doan wan' no peas,
Mama doan wan' no cocoanut oil."

His singing voice was deep and rough and he used the broken groan of the blues singer quite expertly. He moved his body only a little, against rather than in time with the music. The gestures he made with his hands were extremely suggestive.

"Mama doan wan't no gin,
Because gin do make her sin,
Mama doan wan' no glass of gin,
Because it boun' to make her sin,
An' keep her hot and bothered all the day."

He seemed to know what the words meant, or at least his body and his voice seemed to know. When he came to the final chorus, his buttocks writhed and his voice carried a top-heavy load of sexual pain.

Tod and Homer applauded. Adore grabbed the string of his sailboat and circled the yard. He was imitating a tugboat. He tooted several times, then ran off.

"He's just a baby," Mrs. Loomis said proudly, "but he's got loads of talent."

Tod and Homer agreed.

She saw that he was gone again and left hurriedly. They could hear her calling in the brush back of the garage.

"Adore! Adore . . ."

"That's a funny woman," Tod said.

Homer sighed.

"I guess it's hard to get a start in pictures. But Faye is awfully pretty."

Tod agreed. She appeared a moment later in a new flower print dress and picture hat and it was his turn to sigh. She was much more than pretty. She posed, quivering and balanced, on the doorstep and looked down at the two men in the patio. She was smiling, a subtle half-smile uncontaminated by thought. She looked just born, everything moist and fresh, volatile and perfumed. Tod suddenly became very conscious of his dull, insensitive feet bound in dead skin and of his hands, sticky and thick, holding a heavy, rough felt hat.

He tried to get out of going to the pictures with them, but couldn't. Sitting next to her in the dark proved the ordeal he expected it to be. Her self-sufficiency made him squirm and the desire to break its smooth surface with a blow, or at least a sudden obscene gesture, became irresistible.

He began to wonder if he himself didn't suffer from the ingrained, morbid apathy he liked to draw in others. Maybe he could only be galvanized into sensibility and that was why he was chasing Faye.

He left hurriedly, without saying good-bye. He had decided to stop running after her. It was an easy decision to make, but a hard one to carry out. In order to manage it, he fell back on one of the oldest tricks in the very full bag of the intellectual. After all, he told himself, he had drawn her enough times. He shut the portfolio that held the drawings he had made of her, tied it with a string, and put it away in his trunk.

It was a childish trick, hardly worthy of a primitive witch doctor, yet it worked. He was able to avoid her for several months. During this time, he took his pad and pencils on a continuous hunt for other models. He spent his nights at the different Hollywood churches, drawing the worshipers. He visited the "Church of Christ, Physical" where holiness was attained through the constant use of chestweights and spring grips; the "Church Invisible" where fortunes were told and the dead made to find lost objects; the "Tabernacle of the Third Coming" where a woman in male clothing preached the "Crusade Against Salt"; and the "Temple Moderne" under whose glass and chromium roof "Brain-Breathing, the Secret of the Aztecs" was taught.

As he watched these people writhe on the hard seats of their churches, he thought of how well Alessandro Magnasco would dramatize the contrast between their drained-out, feeble bodies and their wild, disordered minds. He would not satirize them as Hogarth or Daumier might, nor would he pity them. He would paint their fury with respect, appreciating its awful, anarchic power and aware that they had it in them to destroy civilization.

One Friday night in the "Tabernacle of the Third Coming," a man near Tod stood up to speak. Although his name most likely was Thompson or Johnson and his home town Sioux City, he had the same countersunk eyes, like the heads of burnished spikes, that a monk by Magnasco might have. He was probably just in from one of the colonies in the desert near Soboba Hot Springs where he had been conning over his soul on a diet of raw fruit and nuts. He was very angry. The message he had brought to the city was one that an illiterate anchorite might have given decadent Rome. It was a crazy jumble of dietary rules, economics and Biblical threats. He claimed to have seen the Tiger of Wrath stalking the walls of the citadel and the Jackal of Lust skulking in the shrubbery, and he connected these omens with "thirty dollars every Thursday" and meat eating.

Tod didn't laugh at the man's rhetoric. He knew it was unimportant. What mattered were his messianic rage and the emotional response of his hearers. They sprang to their feet, shaking their fists and shouting. On the altar someone began to beat a bass drum and soon the entire congregation was singing "Onward Christian Soldiers."

20

As time went on, the relationship between Faye and Homer began to change. She became bored with the life they were leading together and as her boredom deepened, she began to persecute him. At first she did it unconsciously, later maliciously.

Homer realized that the end was in sight even before she did. All he could do to prevent its coming was to increase his servility and his generosity. He waited on her hand and foot. He bought her a coat of summer ermine and a light blue Buick runabout.

His servility was like that of a cringing, clumsy dog, who is always anticipating a blow, welcoming it even, and in a way that makes overwhelming the desire to strike him. His generosity was still more irritating. It was so helpless and unselfish that it made her feel mean and cruel, no matter how hard she tried to be kind. And it was so bulky that she was unable to ignore it. She had to resent it. He was destroying himself, and although he didn't mean it that way, forcing her to accept the blame.

They had almost reached a final crisis when Tod saw them again. Late one night, just as he was preparing for bed, Homer knocked on his door and said that Faye was downstairs in the car and that they wanted him to go to a night club with them.

The outfit Homer wore was very funny. He had on loose blue linen slacks and a chocolate flannel jacket over a yellow polo shirt. Only a Negro could have worn it without looking ridiculous, and no one was ever less a Negro than Homer.

Tod drove with them to the "Cinderella Bar," a little stucco building in the shape of a lady's slipper, on Western Avenue. Its floor show consisted of female impersonators.

Faye was in a nasty mood. When the waiter took their order, she insisted on a champagne cocktail for Homer. He wanted coffee. The waiter brought both, but she made him take the coffee back.

Homer explained painstakingly, as he must have done many times, that he could not drink alcohol because it made him sick. Faye listened with mock patience. When he finished, she laughed and lifted the cocktail to his mouth.

"Drink it, damn you," she said.

She tilted the glass, but he didn't open his mouth and the liquor ran down his chin. He wiped himself, using the napkin without unfolding it.

Faye called the waiter again.

"He doesn't like champagne cocktails," she said. "Bring him brandy."

Homer shook his head.

"Please, Faye," he whimpered.

She held the brandy to his lips, moving the glass when he turned away.

"Come on, sport—bottoms up."

"Let him alone," Tod finally said.

She ignored him as though she hadn't even heard his protest. She was both furious and ashamed of herself. Her shame strengthened her fury and gave it a target.

"Come on, sport," she said savagely, "or mama'll spank."

She turned to Tod.

"I don't like people who won't drink. It isn't sociable. They feel superior and I don't like people who feel superior."

"I don't feel superior," Homer said.

"Oh, yes, you do. I'm drunk and you're sober and so you feel superior. Goddamned, stinking superior."

He opened his mouth to reply and she poured the brandy into it, then clapped her hand over his lips so that he couldn't spit it back. Some of it came out of his nose.

Still without unfolding the napkin, he wiped himself. Faye ordered another brandy. When it came, she held it to his lips again, but this time he took it and drank it himself, fighting the stuff down.

"That's the boy," Faye laughed. "Well done, sloppy-boppy."

Tod asked her to dance in order to give Homer a moment alone. When they reached the floor, she made an attempt to defend herself.

"That guy's superiority is driving me crazy."

"He loves you," Tod said.

"Yeah, I know, but he's such a slob."

She started to cry on his shoulder and he held her very tight. He took a long chance.

"Sleep with me."

"No, baby," she said sympathetically.

"Please, please . . . just once."

"I can't, honey. I don't love you."

"You worked for Mrs. Jenning. Make believe you're still working for her."

She didn't get angry.

"That was a mistake. And anyway, that was different. I only went on call enough times to pay for the funeral and besides those men were complete strangers. You know what I mean?"

"Yes. But please, darling. I'll never bother you again. I'll go east right after. Be kind."

"I can't."

"Why . . . ?"

"I just can't. I'm sorry, darling. I'm not a tease, but I can't like that."

"I love you."

"No, sweetheart, I can't."

They danced until the number finished without saying anything else. He was grateful to her for having behaved so well, for not having made him feel too ridiculous.

When they returned to the table, Homer was sitting exactly as they had left him. He held the folded napkin in one hand and the empty brandy glass in the other. His helplessness was extremely irritating.

"You're right about the brandy, Faye," Homer said. "It's swell! Whoopee!"

He made a little circular gesture with the hand that held the glass.

"I'd like a Scotch," Tod said.

"Me, too," Faye said.

Homer made another gallant attempt to get into the spirit of the evening.

"Garsoon," he called to the waiter, "more drinks."

He grinned at them anxiously. Faye burst out laughing and Homer did his best to laugh with her. When she stopped suddenly, he found himself laughing alone and turned his laugh into a cough, then hid the cough in his napkin.

She turned to Tod.

"What the devil can you do with a slob like that?"

The orchestra started and Tod was able to ignore her question. All three of them turned to watch a young man in a tight evening gown of red silk sing a lullaby.

"Little man, you're crying,
I know why you're blue,
Someone took your kiddycar away;
Better go to sleep now,
Little man, you've had a busy day . . ."

He had a soft, throbbing voice and his gestures were matronly, tender and aborted, a series of unconscious caresses. What he was doing was in no sense parody; it was too simple and too restrained. It wasn't even theatrical. This dark young man with his thin, hairless arms and soft, rounded shoulders, who rocked an imaginary cradle as he crooned, was really a woman.

When he had finished, there was a great deal of applause. The young man shook himself and became an actor again. He tripped on his train, as though he weren't used to it, lifted his skirts to show he was wearing Paris garters, then strode off swinging his shoulders. His imitation of a man was awkward and obscene.

Homer and Tod applauded him.

"I hate fairies," Faye said.

"All women do."

Tod meant it as a joke, but Faye was angry.

"They're dirty," she said.

He started to say something else, but Faye had turned to Homer again. She seemed unable to resist nagging him. This time she pinched his arm until he gave a little squeak.

"Do you know what a fairy is?" she demanded.

"Yes," he said hesitatingly.

"All right, then," she barked. "Give out! What's a fairy?"

Homer twisted uneasily, as though he already felt the ruler on his behind, and looked imploring at Tod, who tried to help him by forming the word "homo" with his lips.

"Momo," Homer said.

Faye burst out laughing. But his hurt look made it impossible not to relent, so she patted his shoulder.

"What a hick," she said.

He grinned gratefully and signaled the waiter to bring another round of drinks.

The orchestra began to play and a man came over to ask Faye to dance. Without saying a word to Homer, she followed him to the floor.

"Who's that?" Homer asked, chasing them with his eyes.

Tod made believe he knew and said that he had often seen him around the San Berdoo. His explanation satisfied Homer, but at the same time set him to thinking of something else. Tod could almost see him shaping a question in his head.

"Do you know Earle Shoop?" Homer finally asked.

"Yes."

Homer then poured out a long, confused story about a dirty black hen. He kept referring to the hen again and again, as though it were the one thing he couldn't stand

about Earle and the Mexican. For a man who was incapable of hatred, he managed to draw a pretty horrible picture of the bird.

"You never saw such a disgusting thing, the way it
squats and turns its head. The roosters have torn all the
feathers off its neck and made its comb all bloody and it
has scabby feet covered with warts and it cackles so nasty
when they drop it into the pen."

"Who drops it into what pen?"

"The Mexican."

"Miguel?"

"Yes. He's almost as bad as his hen."

"You've been to their camp?"

"Camp?"

"In the mountains?"

"No. They're living in the garage. Faye asked me if I
minded if a friend of hers lived in the garage for a while
because he was broke. But I didn't know about the chickens or the Mexican. . . . Lots of people are out of work
nowadays."

"Why don't you throw them out?"

"They're broke and they have no place to go. It isn't
very comfortable living in a garage."

"But if they don't behave?"

"It's just that hen. I don't mind the roosters, they're
pretty, but that dirty hen. She shakes her dirty feathers
each time and clucks so nasty."

"You don't have to look at it."

"They do it every afternoon at the same time when I'm
usually sitting in the chair in the sun after I get back from
shopping with Faye and just before dinner. The Mexican
knows I don't like to see it so he tries to make me look just
for spite. I go into the house, but he taps on the windows
and calls me to come out and watch. I don't call that fun.
Some people have funny ideas of what's fun."

"What's Faye say?"

"She doesn't mind the hen. She says it's only natural."

Then, in case Tod should mistake this for criticism, he told him what a fine, wholesome child she was. Tod agreed, but brought him back to the subject.

"If I were you," he said, "I'd report the chickens to the police. You have to have a permit to keep chickens in the city. I'd do something and damned quick."

Homer avoided a direct answer.

"I wouldn't touch that thing for all the money in the world. She's all over scabs and almost naked. She looks like a buzzard. She eats meat. I saw her one time eating some meat that the Mexican got out of the garbage can. He feeds the roosters grain but the hen eats garbage and he keeps her in a dirty box."

"If I were you, I'd throw those bastards out and their birds with them."

"No, they're nice enough young fellows, just down on their luck, like a lot of people these days, you know. It's just that hen . . ."

He shook his head wearily, as though he could smell and taste her.

Faye was coming back. Homer saw that Tod was going to speak to her about Earle and the Mexican and signaled desperately for him not to do it. She, however, caught him at it and was curious.

"What have you guys been chinning about?"

"You, darling," Tod said. "Homer has a t.l. for you."

"Tell me, Homer."

"No, first you tell me one."

"Well, the man I just danced with asked me if you were a movie big shot."

Tod saw that Homer was unable to think of a return compliment so he spoke for him.

"I said you were the most beautiful girl in the place."

"Yes," Homer agreed. "That's what Tod said."

"I don't believe it. Tod hates me. And anyway, I caught you telling him to keep quiet. You were shushing him."

She laughed.

"I bet I know what you were talking about." She mimicked Homer's excited disgust. " 'That dirty black hen, she's all over scabs and almost naked.' "

Homer laughed apologetically, but Tod was angry.

"What's the idea of keeping those guys in the garage?" he demanded.

"What the hell is it your business?" she replied, but not with real anger. She was amused.

"Homer enjoys their company. Don't you, sloppy-boppy?"

"I told Tod they were nice fellows just down on their luck like a lot of people these days. There's an awful lot of unemployment going around."

"That's right," she said. "If they go, I go."

Tod had guessed as much. He realized there was no use in saying anything. Homer was again signaling for him to keep quiet.

For some reason or other, Faye suddenly became ashamed of herself. She apologized to Tod by offering to dance with him again, flirting as she suggested it. Tod refused.

She broke the silence that followed by a eulogy of Miguel's game chickens, which was really meant to be an excuse for herself. She described what marvelous fighters the birds were, how much Miguel loved them and what good care he took of them.

Homer agreed enthusiastically. Tod remained silent. She asked him if he had ever seen a cock fight and invited him to the garage for the next night. A man from San Diego was coming north with his birds to pit them against Miguel's.

When she turned to Homer again, he leaned away as though she were going to hit him. She flushed with shame at this and looked at Tod to see if he had noticed. The rest of the evening, she tried to be nice to Homer. She even touched him a little, straightening his collar and patting his hair smooth. He beamed happily.

21

When Tod told Claude Estee about the cock fight, he wanted to go with him. They drove to Homer's place together.

It was one of those blue and lavender nights when the luminous color seems to have been blown over the scene with an air brush. Even the darkest shadows held some purple.

A car stood in the driveway of the garage with its headlights on. They could see several men in the corner of the building and could hear their voices. Someone laughed, using only two notes, ha-ha and ha-ha, over and over again.

Tod stepped ahead to make himself known, in case they were taking precautions against the police. When he entered the light, Abe Kusich and Miguel greeted him, but Earle didn't.

"The fights are off," Abe said. "That stinkola from Diego didn't get here."

Claude came up and Tod introduced him to the three men. The dwarf was arrogant, Miguel gracious and Earle his usual wooden, surly self.

Most of the garage floor had been converted into a pit, an oval space about nine feet long and seven or eight wide. It was floored with an old carpet and walled by a low, ragged fence made of odd pieces of lath and wire. Faye's coupe stood in the driveway, placed so that its headlights flooded the arena.

Claude and Tod followed Abe out of the glare and sat down with him on an old trunk in the back of the garage. Earle and Miguel came in and squatted on their heels facing them. They were both wearing blue denims, polka-dot shirts, big hats and high-heeled boots. They looked very handsome and picturesque.

They sat smoking silently, all of them calm except the dwarf, who was fidgety. Although he had plenty of room, he suddenly gave Tod a shove.

"Get over, lard-ass," he snarled.

Tod moved, crowding against Claude, without saying anything. Earle laughed at Tod rather than the dwarf, but the dwarf turned on him anyway.

"Why, you punkola! Who you laughing at?"

"You," Earle said.

"That so, hah? Well, listen to me, you pee-hole bandit, for two cents I'd knock you out of them prop boots."

Earle reached into his shirt pocket and threw a coin on the ground.

"There's a nickel," he said.

The dwarf started to get off the trunk, but Tod caught him by the collar. He didn't try to get loose, but leaned forward against his coat, like a terrier in a harness, and wagged his great head from side to side.

"Go on," he sputtered, "you fugitive from the Western Costume Company, you . . . you louse in a fright-wig, you."

Earle would have been much less angry if he could have thought of a snappy comeback. He mumbled something about a half-pint bastard, then spat. He hit the instep of the dwarf's shoe with a big gob of spittle.

"Nice shot," Miguel said.

This was apparently enough for Earle to consider himself the winner, for he smiled and became quiet. The dwarf slapped Tod's hand away from his collar with a curse and settled down on the trunk again.

"He ought to wear gaffs," Miguel said.

"I don't need them for a punk like that."

They all laughed and everything was fine again.

Abe leaned across Tod to speak to Claude.

"It would have been a swell main," he said. "There was more than a dozen guys here before you come and some of them with real dough. I was going to make book."

He took out his wallet and gave him one of his business cards.

"It was in the bag," Miguel said. "I got five birds that would of won easy and two sure losers. We would of made a killing."

"I've never seen a chicken fight," Claude said. "In fact, I've never even seen a game chicken."

Miguel offered to show him one of his birds and left to get it. Tod went down to the car for the bottle of whiskey they had left in a side pocket. When he got back, Miguel was holding Jujutala in the light. They all examined the bird.

Miguel held the cock firmly with both hands, somewhat in the manner that a basketball is held for an underhand toss. The bird had short, oval wings and a heart-shaped tail that stood at right angles to its body. It had a triangular head, like a snake's, terminating in a slightly curved beak, thick at the base and fine at the point. All its feathers were so tight and hard that they looked as though they had been varnished. They had been thinned out for fighting and the lines of its body, which was like a truncated wedge, stood out plainly. From between Miguel's fingers dangled its long, bright orange legs and its slightly darker feet with their horn nails.

"Juju was bred by John R. Bowes of Lindale, Texas,"

Miguel said proudly. "He's a six times winner. I give fifty dollars and a shotgun for him."

"He's a nice bird," the dwarf said grudgingly, "but looks ain't everything."

Claude took out his wallet.

"I'd like to see him fight," he said. "Suppose you sell me one of your other birds and I put it against him."

Miguel thought a while and looked at Earle, who told him to go ahead.

"I've got a bird I'll sell you for fifteen bucks," he said.

The dwarf interfered.

"Let me pick the bird."

"Oh, I don't care," Claude said, "I just want to see a fight. Here's your fifteen."

Earle took the money and Miguel told him to get Hermano, the big red.

"That red'll go over eight pounds," he said, "while Juju won't go more than six."

Earle came back carrying a large rooster that had a silver shawl. He looked like an ordinary barnyard fowl.

When the dwarf saw him, he became indignant.

"What do you call that, a goose?"

"That's one of Street's Butcher Boys," Miguel said.

"I wouldn't bait a hook with him," the dwarf said.

"You don't have to bet," Earle mumbled.

The dwarf eyed the bird and the bird eyed him. He turned to Claude.

"Let me handle him for you, mister," he said.

Miguel spoke quickly.

"Earle'll do it. He knows the cock."

The dwarf exploded at this.

"It's a frame-up!" he yelled.

He tried to take the red, but Earle held the bird high in the air out of the little man's reach.

Miguel opened the trunk and took out a small wooden

box, the kind chessmen are kept in. It was full of curved gaffs, small squares of chamois with holes in their centers and bits of waxed string like that used by a shoemaker.

They crowded around to watch him arm Juju. First he wiped the short stubs on the cock's legs to make sure they were clean and then placed a leather square over one of them so that the stub came through the hole. He then fitted a gaff over it and fastened it with a bit of the soft string, wrapping very carefully. He did the same to the other leg.

When he had finished, Earle started on the big red.

"That's a bird with lots of cojones," Miguel said. "He's won plenty fights. He don't look fast maybe, but he's fast all right and he packs an awful wallop."

"Strictly for the cook stove, if you ask me," the dwarf said.

Earle took out a pair of shears and started to lighten the red's plumage. The dwarf watched him cut away most of the bird's tail, but when he began to work on the breast, he caught his hand.

"Leave him be!" he barked. "You'll kill him fast that way. He needs that stuff for protection."

He turned to Claude again.

"Please, mister, let me handle him."

"Make him buy a share in the bird," Miguel said.

Claude laughed and motioned for Earle to give Abe the bird. Earle didn't want to and looked meaningly at Miguel.

The dwarf began to dance with rage.

"You're trying to cold-deck us!" he screamed.

"Aw, give it to him," Miguel said.

The little man tucked the bird under his left arm so that his hands were free and began to look over the gaffs in the box. They were all the same length, three inches, but some had more pronounced curves than the others. He selected a pair and explained his strategy to Claude.

"He's going to do most of his fighting on his back. This pair'll hit right that way. If he could get over the other bird, I wouldn't use them."

He got down on his knees and honed the gaffs on the cement floor until they were like needles.

"Have we a chance?" Tod asked.

"You can't ever tell," he said, shaking his extra large head. "He feels almost like a dead bird."

After adjusting the gaffs with great care, he looked the bird over, stretching its wings and blowing its feathers in order to see its skin.

"The comb ain't bright enough for fighting condition," he said, pinching it, "but he looks strong. He may have been a good one once."

He held the bird in the light and looked at its head. When Miguel saw him examining its beak, he told him anxiously to quit stalling. But the dwarf paid no attention and went on muttering to himself. He motioned for Tod and Claude to look.

"What'd I tell you!" he said, puffing with indignation. "We've been cold-decked."

He pointed to a hair line running across the top of the bird's beak.

"That's not a crack," Miguel protested, "it's just a mark."

He reached for the bird as though to rub its beak and the bird pecked savagely at him. This pleased the dwarf.

"We'll fight," he said, "but we won't bet."

Earle was to referee. He took a piece of chalk and drew three lines in the center of the pit, a long one in the middle and two shorter ones parallel to it and about three feet away.

"Pit your cocks," he called.

"No, bill them first," the dwarf protested.

He and Miguel stood at arm's length and thrust their birds together to anger them. Juju caught the big red by the comb and held on viciously until Miguel jerked him away. The red, who had been rather apathetic, came to life and the dwarf had trouble holding him. The two men thrust their birds together again, and again Juju caught the red's comb. The big cock became frantic with rage and struggled to get at the smaller bird.

"We're ready," the dwarf said.

He and Miguel climbed into the pit and set their birds down on the short lines so that they faced each other. They held them by the tails and waited for Earle to give the signal to let go.

"Pit them," he ordered.

The dwarf had been watching Earle's lips and he had his bird off first, but Juju rose straight in the air and sank one spur in the red's breast. It went through the feathers into the flesh. The red turned with the gaff still stuck in him and pecked twice at his opponent's head.

They separated the birds and held them to the lines again.

"Pit 'em!" Earle shouted.

Again Juju got above the other bird, but this time he missed with his spurs. The red tried to get above him, but couldn't. He was too clumsy and heavy to fight in the air. Juju climbed again, cutting and hitting so rapidly that his legs were a golden blur. The red met him by going back on his tail and hooking upward like a cat. Juju landed again and again. He broke one of the red's wings, then practically severed a leg.

"Handle them," Earle called.

When the dwarf gathered the red up, its neck had begun to droop and it was a mass of blood and matted feathers. The little man moaned over the bird, then set to work. He spit into its gaping beak and took the comb between his lips and sucked the blood back into it. The red began to regain its fury, but not its strength. Its beak closed and its neck straightened. The dwarf smoothed and shaped its plumage. He could no nothing to help the broken wing or the dangling leg.

"Pit 'em," Earle said.

The dwarf insisted that the birds be put down beak to beak on the center line, so that the red would not have to move to get at his opponent. Miguel agreed.

The red was very gallant. When Abe let go of its tail, it made a great effort to get off the ground and meet Juju in the air, but it could only thrust with one leg and fell over on its side. Juju sailed above it, half turned and came down on its back, driving in both spurs. The red twisted free, throwing Juju, and made a terrific effort to hook with its good leg, but fell sideways again.

Before Juju could get into the air, the red managed to drive a hard blow with its beak to Juju's head. This slowed the smaller bird down and he fought on the ground. In the pecking match, the red's greater weight and strength evened up for his lack of a leg and a wing. He managed to give as good as he got. But suddenly his cracked beak broke off, leaving only the lower half. A large bubble of blood rose where the beak had been. The red didn't retreat an inch, but made a great effort to get into the air once more. Using its one leg skillfully, it managed to rise six or seven inches from the ground, not enough, however, to get its spurs into play. Juju went up with him and got well above, then drove both gaffs into the red's breast. Again one of the steel needles stuck.

"Handle them," Earle shouted.

Miguel freed his bird and gave the other back to the dwarf. Abe, moaning softly, smoothed its feathers and licked its eyes clean, then took its whole head in his mouth. The red was finished, however. It couldn't even hold its neck straight. The dwarf blew away the feathers from under its tail and pressed the lips of its vent together hard. When that didn't seem to help, he inserted his little finger and scratched the bird's testicles. It fluttered and made a gallant effort to straighten its neck.

"Pit birds."

Once more the red tried to rise with Juju, pushing hard with its remaining leg, but it only spun crazily. Juju rose, but missed. The red thrust weakly with its broken bill. Juju went into the air again and this time drove a gaff through one of the red's eyes into its brain. The red fell over stone dead.

The dwarf groaned with anguish, but no one else said anything. Juju pecked at the dead bird's remaining eye.

"Take off that stinking cannibal!" the dwarf screamed.

Miguel laughed, then caught Juju and removed its gaffs. Earle did the same for the red. He handled the dead cock gently and with respect.

Tod passed the whiskey.

22

They were well on their way to getting drunk when Homer came out to the garage. He gave a little start when he saw the dead chicken sprawled on the carpet. He shook hands with Claude after Tod introduced him, and with Abe Kusich, then made a little set speech about everybody coming in for a drink. They trooped after him.

Faye greeted them at the door. She was wearing a pair of green silk lounging pajamas and green mules with large pompons and very high heels. The top three buttons of her jacket were open and a good deal of her chest was exposed but nothing of her breasts; not because they were small, but because they were placed wide apart and their thrust was upward and outward.

She gave Tod her hand and patted the dwarf on the top of the head. They were old friends. In acknowledging

Homer's awkward introduction of Claude, she was very much the lady. It was her favorite role and she assumed it whenever she met a new man, especially if he were someone whose affluence was obvious.

"Charmed to have you," she trilled.

The dwarf laughed at her.

In a voice stiff with hauteur, she then ordered Homer into the kitchen for soda, ice and glasses.

"A swell layout," announced the dwarf, putting on the hat he had taken off in the doorway.

He climbed into one of the big Spanish chairs, using his knees and hands to do it, and sat on the edge with his feet dangling. He looked like a ventriloquist's dummy.

Earle and Miguel had remained behind to wash up. When they came in, Faye welcomed them with stilted condescension.

"How do you do, boys? The refreshments will be along in a jiffy. But perhaps you prefer a liqueur, Miguel?"

"No, mum," he said, a little startled. "I'll have what the others have."

He followed Earle across the room to the couch. Both of them took long, wooden steps, as though they weren't used to being in a house. They sat down gingerly with their backs straight, their big hats on their knees and their hands under their hats. They had combed their hair before leaving the garage and their small round heads glistened prettily.

Homer took the drinks around on a small tray.

They all made a show of manners, all but the dwarf, that is, who remained as arrogant as ever. He even commented on the quality of the whiskey. As soon as everyone had been served, Homer sat down.

Faye alone remained standing. She was completely self-possessed despite their stares. She stood with one hip thrown out and her hand on it. From where Claude was sitting he could follow the charming line of her spine as it swooped into her buttocks, which were like a heart upside down.

He gave a low whistle of admiration and everyone agreed by moving uneasily or laughing.

"My dear," she said to Homer, "perhaps some of the men would like cigars?"

He was surprised and mumbled something about there being no cigars in the house but that he would go to the store for them if . . . Having to say all this made him unhappy and he took the whiskey around again. He poured very generous shots.

"That's a becoming shade of green," Tod said.

Faye peacocked for them all.

"I thought maybe it was a little gaudy . . . vulgar, you know."

"No," Claude said enthusiastically, "it's stunning."

She repaid him for his compliment by smiling in a peculiar, secret way and running her tongue over her lips. It was one of her most characteristic gestures and very effective. It seemed to promise all sorts of undefined intimacies, yet it was really as simple and automatic as the word thanks. She used it to reward anyone for anything, no matter how unimportant.

Claude made the same mistake Tod had often made and jumped to his feet.

"Won't you sit here?" he said, waving gallantly at his chair.

She accepted by repeating the secret smile and the tongue caress. Claude bowed, but then, realizing that everyone was watching him, added a little mock flourish to make himself less ridiculous. Tod joined them, then Earle and Miguel came over. Claude did the courting while the others stood by and stared at her.

"Do you work in pictures, Mr. Estee?" she asked.

"Yes. You're in pictures, of course?"

Everyone was aware of the begging note in his voice, but no one smiled. They didn't blame him. It was almost impossible to keep that note out when talking to her. Men used it just to say good morning.

"Not exactly, but I hope to be," she said. "I've worked as an extra, but I haven't had a real chance yet. I expect to get one soon. All I ask is a chance. Acting is in my blood. We Greeners, you know, were all theatre people from away back."

"Yes. I . . ."

She didn't let Claude finish, but he didn't care.

"Not musicals, but real dramas. Of course, maybe light comedies at first. All I ask is a chance. I've been buying a lot of clothes lately to make myself one. I don't believe in luck. Luck is just hard work, they say, and I'm willing to work as hard as anybody."

"You have a delightful voice and you handle it well," he said.

He couldn't help it. Having once seen her secret smile and the things that accompanied it, he wanted to make her repeat it again and again.

"I'd like to do a show on Broadway," she continued. "That's the way to get a start nowadays. They won't talk to you unless you've had stage experience."

She went on and on, telling him how careers are made in the movies and how she intended to make hers. It was all nonsense. She mixed bits of badly understood advice from the trade papers with other bits out of the fan magazines and compared these with the legends that surround the activities of screen stars and executives. Without any noticeable transition, possibilities became probabilities and wound up as inevitabilities. At first she occasionally stopped and waited for Claude to chorus a hearty agreement, but when she had a good start, all her questions were rhetorical and the stream of words rippled on without a break.

None of them really heard her. They were all too busy watching her smile, laugh, shiver, whisper, grow indignant, cross and uncross her legs, stick out her tongue, widen and narrow her eyes, toss her head so that her platinum hair splashed against the red plush of the chair back. The strange thing about her gestures and expressions was that they didn't really illustrate what she was saying. They were almost pure. It was as though her body recognized how foolish her words were and tried to excite her hearers into being uncritical. It worked that night; no one even thought of laughing at her. The only move they made was to narrow their circle about her.

Tod stood on the outer edge, watching her through the opening between Earle and the Mexican. When he felt a light tap on his shoulder, he knew it was Homer, but didn't turn. When the tap was repeated, he shrugged the hand away. A few minutes later, he heard a shoe squeak behind him and turned to see Homer tiptoeing off. He reached a chair safely and sank into it with a sigh. He put his heavy hands on the knees, one on each, and stared for a while at their backs. He felt Tod's eyes on him and looked up and smiled.

His smile annoyed Tod. It was one of those irritating smiles that seem to say: "My friend, what can you know of suffering?" There was something very patronizing and superior about it, and intolerably snobbish.

He felt hot and a little sick. He turned his back on Homer and went out the front door. His indignant exit wasn't very successful. He wobbled quite badly and when he reached the sidewalk, he had to sit down on the curb with his back against a date palm.

From where he was sitting, he couldn't see the city in the valley below the canyon, but he could see the reflection of its lights, which hung in the sky above it like a batik parasol. The unlighted part of the sky at the edge of the parasol was a deep black with hardly a trace of blue.

Homer followed him out of the house and stood standing behind him, afraid to approach. He might have sneaked away without Tod's knowing it, if he had not suddenly looked down and seen his shadow.

"Hello," he said.

He motioned for Homer to join him on the curb.

"You'll catch cold," Homer said.

Tod understood his protest. He made it because he wanted to be certain that his company was really welcome. Nevertheless, Tod refused to repeat the invitation. He didn't even turn to look at him again. He was sure he was wearing his long-suffering smile and didn't want to see it.

He wondered why all his sympathy had turned to malice. Because of Faye? It was impossible for him to admit it. Because he was unable to do anything to help him? This reason was a more comfortable one, but he dismissed it with even less consideration. He had never set himself up as a healer.

Homer was looking the other way, at the house, watching the parlor window. He cocked his head to one side when someone laughed. The four short sounds, ha-ha and again ha-ha, distinct musical notes, were made by the dwarf.

"You could learn from him," Tod said.

"What?" Homer asked, turning to look at him.

"Let it go."

His impatience both hurt and puzzled Homer. He saw that and motioned for him to sit down, this time emphatically.

Homer obeyed. He did a poor job of squatting and hurt himself. He sat nursing his knee.

"What is it?" Tod finally said, making an attempt to be kind.

"Nothing, Tod, nothing."

He was grateful and increased his smile. Tod couldn't help seeing all its annoying attributes, resignation, kindliness, and humility.

They sat quietly, Homer with his heavy shoulders hunched and the sweet grin on his face, Tod frowning, his back pressed hard against the palm tree. In the house the radio was playing and its blare filled the street.

They sat for a long time without speaking. Several times Homer started to tell Tod something but he didn't seem able to get the words out. Tod refused to help him with a question.

His big hands left his lap, where they had been playing "here's the church and here the steeple," and hid in his armpits. They remained there for a moment, then slid under his thighs. A moment later they were back in his lap. The right hand cracked the joints of the left, one by one, then the left did the same service for the right. They seemed easier for a moment, but not for long. They started "here's the church" again, going through the entire performance and ending with the joint manipulation as before. He started a third time, but catching Tod's eyes, he stopped and trapped his hands between his knees.

It was the most complicated tic Tod had ever seen. What made it particularly horrible was its precision. It wasn't pantomime, as he had first thought, but manual ballet.

When Tod saw the hands start to crawl out again, he exploded.

"For Christ's sake!"

The hands struggled to get free, but Homer clamped his knees shut and held them.

"I'm sorry," he said.

"Oh, all right."

"But I can't help it, Tod. I have to do it three times."

"Okay with me."

He turned his back on him.

Faye started to sing and her voice poured into the street.

"Dreamed about a reefer five feet long
Not too mild and not too strong,
You'll be high, but not for long,
If you're a viper—a vi-paah."

Instead of her usual swing delivery, she was using a lugubrious one, wailing the tune as though it were a dirge. At the end of every stanza, she shifted to an added minor.

"I'm the queen of everything,
Gotta be high before I can swing,
Light a tea and let it be,
If you're a viper—a vi-paah."

"She sings very pretty," Homer said.

"She's drunk."

"I don't know what to do, Tod," Homer complained. "She's drinking an awful lot lately. It's that Earle. We used to have a lot of fun before he came, but now we don't have any fun any more since he started to hang around."

"Why don't you get rid of him?"

"I was thinking about what you said about the license to keep chickens."

Tod understood what he wanted.

"I'll report them to the Board of Health tomorrow."

Homer thanked him, then insisted on explaining in detail why he couldn't do it himself.

"But that'll only get rid of the Mexican," Tod said. "You'll have to throw Earle out yourself."

"Maybe he'll go with his friend?"

Tod knew that Homer was begging him to agree so that he could go on hoping, but he refused.

"Not a chance. You'll have to throw him out."

Homer accepted this with his brave, sweet smile.

"Maybe . . ."

"Tell Faye to do it," Tod said.

"Oh, I can't."

"Why the hell not? It's your house."

"Don't be mad at me, Toddie."

"All right, Homie, I'm not mad at you."

Faye's voice came through the open window.

"And when your throat gets dry,
You know you're high,
If you're a viper."

The others harmonized on the last word, repeating it.

"Vi-paah . . ."

"Toddie," Homer began, "if . . ."

"Stop calling me Toddie, for Christ's sake!"

Homer didn't understand. He took Tod's hand.

"I didn't mean nothing. Back home we call . . ."

Tod couldn't stand his trembling signals of affection. He tore free with a jerk.

"Oh, but, Toddie, I . . ."

"She's a whore!"

He heard Homer grunt, then heard his knees creak as he struggled to his feet.

Faye's voice came pouring through the window, a reedy wail that broke in the middle with a husky catch.

"High, high, high, high, when you're high,
Everything is dandy,
Truck on down to the candy store,
Bust your conk on peppermint candy!
Then you know your body's sent,
Don't care if you don't pay rent,
Sky is high and so am I,
If you're a viper—a vi-paah."

23

When Tod went back into the house, he found Earle, Abe Kusich and Claude standing together in a tight group, watching Faye dance with Miguel. She and the Mexican were doing a slow tango to music from the phonograph. He held her very tight, one of his legs thrust between hers, and they swayed together in long spirals that broke rhythmically at the top of each curve into a dip. All the buttons on her lounging pajamas were open and the arm he had around her waist was inside her clothes.

Tod stood watching the dancers from the doorway for a moment, then went to a little table on which the whiskey bottle was. He poured himself a quarter of a tumblerful, tossed it off, then poured another drink. Carrying the glass, he went over to Claude and the others. They paid no attention to him; their heads moved only to follow the dancers, like the gallery at a tennis match.

"Did you see Homer?" Tod asked, touching Claude's arm.

Claude didn't turn, but the dwarf did. He spoke as though hypnotized.

"What a quiff! What a quiff!"

Tod left them and went to look for Homer. He wasn't in the kitchen, so he tried the bedrooms. One of them was locked. He knocked lightly, waited, then repeated the knock. There was no answer, but he thought he heard

someone move. He looked through the keyhole. The room
was pitch dark.

"Homer," he called softly.

He heard the bed creak, then Homer replied.

"Who is it?"

"It's me—Toddie."

He used the diminutive with perfect seriousness.

"Go away, please," Homer said.

"Let me in for a minute. I want to explain something."

"No," Homer said, "go away, please."

Tod went back to the living room. The phonograph
record had been changed to a fox-trot and Earle was
now dancing with Faye. He had both his arms around
her in a bear hug and they were stumbling all over the
room, bumping into the walls and furniture. Faye, her head
thrown back, was laughing wildly. Earle had both eyes shut
tight.

Miguel and Claude were also laughing, but not the
dwarf. He stood with his fists clenched and his chin stuck
out. When he couldn't stand any more of it, he ran after
the dancers to cut in. He caught Earle by the seat of his
trousers.

"Le'me dance," he barked.

Earle turned his head, looking down at the dwarf from
over his shoulder.

"Git! G'wan, git!"

Faye and Earle had come to a halt with their arms
around each other. When the dwarf lowered his head
like a goat and tried to push between them, she reached
down and tweaked his nose.

"Le'me dance," he bellowed.

They tried to start again, but Abe wouldn't let them.
He had his hands between them and was trying frantically
to pull them apart. When that wouldn't work, he kicked
Earle sharply in the shins. Earle kicked back and his boot

landed in the little man's stomach, knocking him flat on his back. Everyone laughed.

The dwarf struggled to his feet and stood with his head lowered like a tiny ram. Just as Faye and Earle started to dance again, he charged between Earle's legs and dug upward with both hands. Earle screamed with pain, and tried to get at him. He screamed again, then groaned and started to sink to the floor, tearing Faye's silk pajamas on his way down.

Miguel grabbed Abe by the throat. The dwarf let go his hold and Earle sank to the floor. Lifting the little man free, Miguel shifted his grip to his ankles and dashed him against the wall, like a man killing a rabbit against a tree. He swung the dwarf back to slam him again, but Tod caught his arm. Then Claude grabbed the dwarf and together they pulled him away from the Mexican.

He was unconscious. They carried him into the kitchen and held him under the cold water. He came to quickly and began to curse. When they saw he was all right, they went back to the living room.

Miguel was helping Earle over to the couch. All the tan had drained from his face and it was covered with sweat. Miguel loosened his trousers while Claude took off his necktie and opened his collar.

Faye and Tod watched from the side.

"Look," she said, "my new pajamas are ruined."

One of the sleeves had been pulled almost off and her shoulder stuck through it. The trousers were also torn. While he stared at her, she undid the top of the trousers and stepped out of them. She was wearing tight black lace drawers. Tod took a step toward her and hesitated. She threw the pajama bottoms over her arm, turned slowly and walked toward the door.

"Faye," Tod gasped.

She stopped and smiled at him.

"I'm going to bed," she said. "Get that little guy out of here."

Claude came over and took Tod by the arm.

"Let's blow," he said.

Tod nodded.

"We'd better take the homunculus with us or he's liable to murder the whole household."

Tod nodded again and followed him into the kitchen. They found the dwarf holding a big piece of ice to the side of his head.

"There's some lump where that greaser slammed me."

He made them finger and admire it.

"Let's go home," Claude said.

"No," said the dwarf, "let's go see some girls. I'm just getting started."

"To hell with that," snapped Tod. "Come on."

He pushed the dwarf toward the door.

"Take your hands off, punk!" roared the little man.

Claude stepped between them.

"Easy there, citizen," he said.

"All right, but no shoving."

He strutted out and they followed.

Earle still lay stretched on the couch. He had his eyes closed and was holding himself below the stomach with both hands. Miguel wasn't there.

Abe chuckled, wagging his big head gleefully.

"I fixed that buckeroo."

Out on the sidewalk he tried again to get them to go with him.

"Come on, you guys—we'll have some fun."

"I'm going home," Claude said.

They went with the dwarf to his car and watched him climb in behind the wheel. He had special extensions on the clutch and brake so that he could reach them with his tiny feet.

"Come to town?"

"No, thanks," Claude said politely.

"Then to hell with you!"

That was his farewell. He let out the brake and the car rolled away.

24

Tod woke up the next morning with a splitting headache. He called the studio to say he wouldn't be in and remained in bed until noon, then went downtown for breakfast. After several cups of hot tea, he felt a little better and decided to visit Homer. He still wanted to apologize.

Climbing the hill to Pinyon Canyon made his head throb and he was relieved when no one answered his repeated knocks. As he started away, he saw one of the curtains move and went back to knock once more. There was still no answer.

He went around to the garage. Faye's car was gone and so were the game chickens. He went to the back of the house and knocked on the kitchen door. Somehow the silence seemed too complete. He tried the handle and found that the door wasn't locked. He shouted hello a few times, as a warning, then went through the kitchen into the living room.

The red velvet curtains were all drawn tight, but he could see Homer sitting on the couch and staring at the backs of his hands which were cupped over his knees. He wore an old-fashioned cotton nightgown and his feet were bare.

"Just get up?"

Homer neither moved nor replied.

Tod tried again.

"Some party!"

He knew it was stupid to be hearty, but he didn't know what else to be.

"Boy, have I got a hang-over," he went on, even going so far as to attempt a chuckle.

Homer paid absolutely no attention to him.

The room was just as they had left it the night before. Tables and chairs were overturned and the smashed picture lay where it had fallen. To give himself a reason for staying, he began to tidy up. He righted the chairs, straightened the carpet and picked up the cigarette butts that littered the floor. He also threw aside the curtains and opened a window.

"There, that's better, isn't it?" he asked cheerfully.

Homer looked up for a second, then down at his hands again. Tod saw that he was coming out of his stupor.

"Want some coffee?" he asked.

He lifted his hands from his knees and hid them in his armpits, clamping them tight, but didn't answer.

"Some hot coffee—what do you say?"

He took his hands from under his arms and sat on them. After waiting a little while he shook his head no, slowly, heavily, like a dog with a foxtail in its ear.

"I'll make some."

Tod went to the kitchen and put the pot on the stove. While it was boiling, he took a peek into Faye's room. It had been stripped. All the dresser drawers were pulled out and there were empty boxes all over the floor. A broken flask of perfume lay in the middle of the carpet and the place reeked of gardenia.

When the coffee was ready, he poured two cups and carried them into the living room on a tray. He found Homer just as he had left him, sitting on his hands. He moved a small table close to him and put the tray on it.

"I brought a cup for myself, too," he said. "Come on—drink it while it's hot."

Tod lifted a cup and held it out, but when he saw that he was going to speak, he put it down and waited.

"I'm going back to Wayneville," Homer said.

"A swell idea—great!"

He pushed the coffee at him again. Homer ignored it. He gulped several times, trying to swallow something that was stuck in his throat, then began to sob. He cried without covering his face or bending his head. The sound was like an ax chopping pine, a heavy, hollow, chunking noise. It was repeated rhythmically but without accent. There was no progress in it. Each chunk was exactly like the one that preceded. It would never reach a climax.

Tod realized that there was no use trying to stop him. Only a very stupid man would have the courage to try to do it. He went to the farthest corner of the room and waited.

Just as he was about to light a second cigarette, Homer called him.

"Tod!"

"I'm here, Homer."

He hurried over to the couch again.

Homer was still crying, but he suddenly stopped even more abruptly than he had started.

"Yes, Homer?" Tod asked encouragingly.

"She's left."

"Yes, I know. Drink some coffee."

"She's left."

Tod knew that he put a great deal of faith in sayings, so he tried one.

"Good riddance to bad rubbish."

"She left before I got up," he said.

"What the hell do you care? You're going back to Wayneville."

"You shouldn't curse," Homer said with the same lunatic calm.

"I'm sorry," Tod mumbled.

The word "sorry" was like dynamite set off under a dam. Language leaped out of Homer in a muddy, twisting torrent. At first, Tod thought it would do him a lot of good to pour out in this way. But he was wrong. The lake behind the dam replenished itself too fast. The more he talked the greater the pressure grew because the flood was circular and ran back behind the dam again.

After going on continuously for about twenty minutes, he stopped in the middle of a sentence. He leaned back, closed his eyes and seemed to fall asleep. Tod put a cushion under his head. After watching him for a while, he went back to the kitchen.

He sat down and tried to make sense out of what Homer had told him. A great deal of it was gibberish. Some of it, however, wasn't. He hit on a key that helped when he realized that a lot of it wasn't jumbled so much as timeless. The words went behind each other instead of after. What he had taken for long strings were really one thick word and not a sentence. In the same way several sentences were simultaneous and not a paragraph. Using this key, he was able to arrange a part of what he had heard so that it made the usual kind of sense.

After Tod had hurt him by saying that nasty thing about Faye, Homer ran around to the back of the house and let himself in through the kitchen, then went to peek into the parlor. He wasn't angry with Tod, just surprised and upset because Tod was a nice boy. From the hall that led into the parlor he could see everybody having a good time and he was glad because it was kind of dull for Faye living with an old man like him. It made her restless. No one noticed him peeking there and he was glad because he didn't feel much like joining the fun, although he liked to watch people enjoy themselves. Faye was dancing with Mr. Estee and they made a nice pair. She seemed happy. Her face

shone like always when she was happy. Next she danced
with Earle. He didn't like that because of the way he
held her. He couldn't see what she saw in that fellow. He
just wasn't nice, that's all. He had mean eyes. In the hotel
business they used to watch out for fellows like that and
never gave them credit because they would jump their
bills. Maybe he couldn't get a job because nobody would
trust him, although it was true as Faye said that a lot of
people were out of work nowadays. Standing there peeking
at the party, enjoying the laughing and singing, he saw
Earle catch Faye and bend her back and kiss her and
everybody laughed although you could see Faye didn't like
it because she slapped his face. Earle didn't care, he just
kissed her again, a long nasty one. She got away from him
and ran toward the door where he was standing. He tried
to hide, but she caught him. Although he didn't say anything, she said he was nasty spying on her and wouldn't
listen when he tried to explain. She went into her room
and he followed to tell about the peeking, but she carried
on awful and cursed him some more as she put red on her
lips. Then she knocked over the perfume. That made her
twice as mad. He tried to explain but she wouldn't listen
and just went on calling him all sorts of dirty things. So he
went to his room and got undressed and tried to go to
sleep. Then Tod woke him up and wanted to come in and
talk. He wasn't angry, but didn't feel like talking just then,
all he wanted to do was go to sleep. Tod went away and
no sooner had he climbed back into bed when there was
some awful screaming and banging. He was afraid to go
out and see and he thought of calling the police, but he
was scared to go in the hall where the phone was so he
started to get dressed to climb out of the window and go
for help because it sounded like murder but before he
finished putting his shoes on, he heard Tod talking to Faye
and he figured that it must be all right or she wouldn't be

laughing so he got undressed and went back to bed again. He couldn't fall asleep wondering what had happened, so when the house was quiet, he took a chance and knocked on Faye's door to find out. Faye let him in. She was curled up in bed like a little girl. She called him daddy and kissed him and said that she wasn't angry at him at all. She said there had been a fight but nobody got hurt much and for him to go back to bed and that they would talk more in the morning. He went back like she said and fell asleep, but he woke up again as it was just breaking daylight. At first he wondered why he was up because when he once fell asleep, usually he didn't get up before the alarm clock rang. He knew that something had happened, but he didn't know what until he heard a noise in Faye's room. It was a moan and he thought he was dreaming, but he heard it again. Sure enough, Faye was moaning all right. He thought she must be sick. She moaned again like in pain. He got out of bed and went to her door and knocked and asked if she was sick. She didn't answer and the moaning stopped so he went back to bed. A little later, she moaned again so he got out of bed, thinking she might want the hot water bottle or some aspirin and a drink of water or something and knocked on her door again, only meaning to help her. She heard him and said something. He didn't understand what but he thought she meant for him to go in. Lots of times when she had a headache he brought her an aspirin and a glass of water in the middle of the night. The door wasn't locked. You'd have thought she would have locked the door because the Mexican was in bed with her, both of them naked and she had her arms around him. Faye saw him and pulled the sheets over her head without saying anything. He didn't know what to do, so he backed out of the room and closed the door. He was standing in the hall, trying to figure out what to do, feeling so ashamed, when Earle appeared with his boots in his hand. He must have been sleeping in the parlor. He wanted to know what the trouble was. "Faye's sick," he said, "and I'm getting her a glass of water." But then Faye moaned again and Earle heard it. He pushed open the door. Faye screamed. He could hear Earl and Miguel cursing each other and fighting. He was afraid to call the police on account of Faye and didn't know what to do. Faye kept on screaming. When he opened the door again, Miguel fell out with Earle on top of him and both of them tearing at each other. He ran inside the room and locked the door. She had the sheets over her head, screaming. He could hear Earle and Miguel fighting in the hall and then he couldn't hear them any more. She kept the sheets over her head. He tried to talk to her but she wouldn't answer. He sat down on a chair to guard her in case Earle and Miguel came back, but they didn't and after a while she pulled the sheets away from her face and told him to get out. She pulled the sheets over her face again when he answered, so then he waited a little longer and again she told him to get out without letting him see her face. He couldn't hear either Miguel or Earle. He opened the door and looked out. They were gone. He locked the doors and windows and went to his room and lay down on his bed. Before he knew it he fell asleep and when he woke up she was gone. All he could find was Earle's boots in the hall. He threw them out the back and this morning they were gone.

25

Tod went into the living room to see how Homer was getting on. He was still on the couch, but had changed his position. He had curled his big body into a ball. His knees were drawn up almost to his chin, his elbows were tucked in close and his hands were against his chest. But he wasn't relaxed. Some inner force of nerve and muscle was straining to make the ball tighter and still tighter. He was like a steel spring which has been freed of its function in a machine and allowed to use all its strength centripetally. While part of a machine the pull of the spring had been used against other and stronger forces, but now, free at last, it was striving to attain the shape of its original coil.

Original coil . . . In a book of abnormal psychology borrowed from the college library, he had once seen a picture of a woman sleeping in a net hammock whose posture was much like Homer's. "Uterine Flight," or something like that, had been the caption under the photograph. The woman had been sleeping in the hammock without changing her position, that of the foetus in the womb, for a great many years. The doctors of the insane asylum had been able to awaken her for only short periods of time and those months apart.

He sat down to smoke a cigarette and wondered what he ought to do. Call a doctor? But after all Homer had been awake most of the night and was exhausted. The doctor would shake him a few times and he would yawn and ask what the matter was. He could try to wake him up himself. But hadn't he been enough of a pest already? He was so much better off asleep, even if it was a case of "Uterine Flight."

What a perfect escape the return to the womb was. Better by far than Religion or Art or the South Sea Islands. It was so snug and warm there, and the feeding was automatic. Everything perfect in that hotel. No wonder the memory of those accommodations lingered in the blood and nerves of everyone. It was dark, yes, but what a warm, rich darkness. The grave wasn't in it. No wonder one fought so desperately against being evicted when the nine months' lease was up.

Tod crushed his cigarette. He was hungry and wanted his dinner, also a double Scotch and soda. After he had eaten, he would come back and see how Homer was. If he was still asleep, he would try to wake him. If he couldn't, he might call a doctor.

He took another look at him, then tiptoed out of the cottage, shutting the door carefully.

26

Tod didn't go directly to dinner. He went first to Hodge's saddlery store thinking he might be able to find out something about Earle and through him about Faye. Calvin was standing there with a wrinkled Indian who had long hair held by a bead strap around his forehead. Hanging over the Indian's chest was a sandwich board that read—

TUTTLE'S TRADING POST

for

GENUINE RELICS OF THE OLD WEST

Beads, Silver, Jewelry, Moccasins,

Dolls, Toys, Rare Books, Postcards.

TAKE BACK A SOUVENIR

from

TUTTLE'S TRADING POST

Calvin was always friendly.

" 'Lo, thar," he called out, when Tod came up.

"Meet the chief," he added, grinning. "Chief Kiss-My-Towkus."

The Indian laughed heartily at the joke.

"You gotta live," he said.

"Earle been around today?" Tod asked.

"Yop. Went by an hour ago."

"We were at a party last night and I . . ."

Calvin broke in by hitting his thigh a wallop with the flat of his palm.

"That must've been some shindig to hear Earle tell it. Eh, Skookum?"

"Vas you dere, Sharley?" the Indian agreed, showing the black inside of his mouth, purple tongue and broken orange teeth.

"I heard there was a fight after I left."

Calvin smacked his thigh again.

"Sure musta been. Earle get himself two black eyes, lulus."

"That's what comes of palling up with a dirty greaser," said the Indian excitedly.

He and Calvin got into a long argument about Mexicans. The Indian said that they were all bad. Calvin claimed he had known quite a few good ones in his time. When the Indian cited the case of the Hermanos brothers who had killed a lonely prospector for half a dollar, Calvin countered with a long tale about a man called Tomas Lopez who shared his last pint of water with a stranger when they both were lost in the desert.

Tod tried to get the conversation back to what interested him.

"Mexicans are very good with women," he said.

"Better with horses," said the Indian. "I remember one time along the Brazos, I . . ."

Tod tried again.

"They fought over Earle's girl, didn't they?"

"Not to hear him tell it," Calvin said. "He claims it was dough—claims the Mex robbed him while he was sleeping."

"The dirty, thievin' rat," said the Indian, spitting.

"He claims he's all washed up with that bitch," Calvin went on. "Yes, siree, that's his story, to hear him tell it."

Tod had enough.

"So long," he said.

"Glad to meet you," said the Indian.

"Don't take any wooden nickels," Calvin shouted after him.

Tod wondered if she had gone with Miguel. He thought it more likely that she would go back to work for Mrs. Jenning. But either way she would come out all right. Nothing could hurt her. She was like a cork. No matter how rough the sea got, she would go dancing over the same waves that sank iron ships and tore away piers of reinforced concrete. He pictured her riding a tremendous sea. Wave after wave reared its ton on ton of solid water and crashed down only to have her spin gaily away.

When he arrived at Musso Frank's restaurant, he ordered a steak and a double Scotch. The drink came first and he sipped it with his inner eye still on the spinning cork.

It was a very pretty cork, gilt with a glittering fragment of mirror set in its top. The sea in which it danced was beautiful, green in the trough of the waves and silver at their tips. But for all their moondriven power, they could do no more than net the bright cork for a moment in a spume of intricate lace. Finally it was set down on a strange shore where a savage with pork-sausage fingers and a pimpled butt picked it up and hugged it to his sagging belly. Tod recognized the fortunate man; he was one of Mrs. Jenning's customers.

The waiter brought his order and paused with bent back for him to comment. In vain. Tod was far too busy to inspect the steak.

"Satisfactory, sir?" asked the waiter.

Tod waved him away with a gesture more often used on flies. The waiter disappeared. Tod tried the same gesture on what he felt, but the driving itch refused to go. If only he had the courage to wait for her some night and hit her with a bottle and rape her.

He knew what it would be like lurking in the dark in a vacant lot, waiting for her. Whatever that bird was that sang at night in California would be bursting its heart in theatrical runs and quavers and the chill night air would smell of spice pink. She would drive up, turn the motor off, look up at the stars, so that her breasts reared, then toss her head and sigh. She would throw the ignition keys into her purse and snap it shut, then get out of the car. The long step she took would make her tight dress pull up so that an inch of glowing flesh would show above her black stocking. As he approached carefully, she would be pulling her dress down, smoothing it nicely over her hips.

"Faye, Faye, just a minute," he would call.

"Why, Tod, hello."

She would hold her hand out to him at the end of her long arm that swooped so gracefully to join her curving shoulder.

"You scared me!"

She would look like a deer on the edge of the road when a truck comes unexpectedly around a bend.

He could feel the cold bottle he held behind his back and the forward step he would take to bring . . .

"Is there anything wrong with it, sir?"

The fly-like waiter had come back. Tod waved at him, but this time the man continued to hover.

"Perhaps you would like me to take it back, sir?"

"No, no."

"Thank you, sir."

But he didn't leave. He waited to make sure that the

customer was really going to eat. Tod picked up his knife and cut a piece. Not until he had also put some boiled potato in his mouth did the man leave.

Tod tried to start the rape going again, but he couldn't feel the bottle as he raised it to strike. He had to give it up.

The waiter came back. Tod looked at the steak. It was a very good one, but he wasn't hungry any more.

"A check, please."

"No dessert, sir?"

"No, thank you, just a check."

"Check it is, sir," the man said brightly as he fumbled for his pad and pencil.

27

When Tod reached the street, he saw a dozen great violet shafts of light moving across the evening sky in wide crazy sweeps. Whenever one of the fiery columns reached the lowest point of its arc, it lit for a moment the rose-colored domes and delicate minarets of Kahn's Persian Palace Theatre. The purpose of this display was to signal the world premiere of a new picture.

Turning his back on the searchlights, he started in the opposite direction, toward Homer's place. Before he had gone very far, he saw a clock that read a quarter past six and changed his mind about going back just yet. He might as well let the poor fellow sleep for another hour and kill some time by looking at the crowds.

When still a block from the theatre, he saw an enormous electric sign that hung over the middle of the street. In letters ten feet high he read that—

"MR. KAHN A PLEASURE DOME DECREED"

Although it was still several hours before the celebrities would arrive, thousands of people had already gathered.

They stood facing the theatre with their backs toward the gutter in a thick line hundreds of feet long. A big squad of policemen was trying to keep a lane open between the front rank of the crowd and the façade of the theatre.

Tod entered the lane while the policeman guarding it was busy with a woman whose parcel had torn open, dropping oranges all over the place. Another policeman shouted for him to get the hell across the street, but he took a chance and kept going. They had enough to do without chasing him. He noticed how worried they looked and how careful they tried to be. If they had to arrest some-one, they joked good-naturedly with the culprit, making light of it until they got him around the corner, then they whaled him with their clubs. Only so long as the man was actually part of the crowd did they have to be gentle.

Tod had walked only a short distance along the narrow lane when he began to get frightened. People shouted, commenting on his hat, his carriage, and his clothing. There was a continuous roar of catcalls, laughter and yells, pierced occasionally by a scream. The scream was usually followed by a sudden movement in the dense mass and part of it would surge forward wherever the police line was weakest. As soon as that part was rammed back, the bulge would pop out somewhere else.

The police force would have to be doubled when the stars started to arrive. At the sight of their heroes and heroines, the crowd would turn demoniac. Some little gesture, either too pleasing or too offensive, would start it moving and then nothing but machine guns would stop it. Individually the purpose of its members might simply be to get a souvenir, but collectively it would grab and rend.

A young man with a portable microphone was describing the scene. His rapid, hysterical voice was like that of a revivalist preacher whipping his congregation toward the ecstasy of fits.

"What a crowd, folks! What a crowd! There must be ten thousand excited, screaming fans outside Kahn's Persian tonight. The police can't hold them. Here, listen to them roar."

He held the microphone out and those near it obligingly roared for him.

"Did you hear it? It's a bedlam, folks. A veritable bedlam! What excitement! Of all the premières I've attended, this is the most . . . the most . . . stupendous, folks. Can the police hold them? Can they? It doesn't look so, folks . . ."

Another squad of police came charging up. The sergeant pleaded with the announcer to stand further back so the people couldn't hear him His men threw themselves at the crowd. It allowed itself to be hustled and shoved out of habit and because it lacked an objective. It tolerated the police, just as a bull elephant does when he allows a small boy to drive him with a light stick.

Tod could see very few people who looked tough, nor could he see any working men. The crowd was made up of the lower middle classes, every other person one of his torchbearers.

Just as he came near the end of the lane, it closed in front of him with a heave, and he had to fight his way through. Someone knocked his hat off and when he stooped to pick it up, someone kicked him. He whirled around angrily and found himself surrounded by people who were laughing at him. He knew enough to laugh with them. The crowd became sympathetic. A stout woman slapped him on the back, while a man handed him his hat, first brushing it carefully with his sleeve. Still another man shouted for a way to be cleared.

By a great deal of pushing and squirming, always trying to look as though he were enjoying himself, Tod finally managed to break into the open. After rearranging his clothes, he went over to a parking lot and sat down on the low retaining wall that ran along the front of it.

New groups, whole families, kept arriving. He could see a change come over them as soon as they had become part of the crowd. Until they reached the line, they looked diffident, almost furtive, but the moment they had become part of it, they turned arrogant and pugnacious. It was a mistake to think them harmless curiosity seekers. They were savage and bitter, especially the middle-aged and the old, and had been made so by boredom and disappointment.

All their lives they had slaved at some kind of dull, heavy labor, behind desks and counters, in the fields and at tedious machines of all sorts, saving their pennies and dreaming of the leisure that would be theirs when they had enough. Finally that day came. They could draw a weekly income of ten or fifteen dollars. Where else should they go but California, the land of sunshine and oranges?

Once there, they discover that sunshine isn't enough. They get tired of oranges, even of avocado pears and passion fruit. Nothing happens. They don't know what to do with their time. They haven't the mental equipment for leisure, the money nor the physical equipment for pleasure. Did they slave so long just to go to an occasional Iowa picnic? What else is there? They watch the waves come in at Venice. There wasn't any ocean where most of them came from, but after you've seen one wave, you've seen them all. The same is true of the airplanes at Glendale. If only a plane would crash once in a while so that they could watch the passengers being consumed in a "holocaust of flame," as the newspapers put it. But the planes never crash.

Their boredom becomes more and more terrible. They realize that they've been tricked and burn with resentment. Every day of their lives they read the newspapers and went to the movies. Both fed them on lynchings, murder, sex crimes, explosions, wrecks, love nests, fires, miracles, revolutions, war. This daily diet made sophisticates of them. The sun is a joke. Oranges can't titillate their jaded palates. Nothing can ever be violent enough to make taut their slack minds and bodies. They have been cheated and betrayed. They have slaved and saved for nothing.

Tod stood up. During the ten minutes he had been sitting on the wall, the crowd had grown thirty feet and he was afraid that his escape might be cut off if he loitered much longer. He crossed to the other side of the street and started back.

He was trying to figure what to do if he were unable to wake Homer when, suddenly he saw his head bobbing above the crowd. He hurried toward him. From his appearance, it was evident that there was something definitely wrong.

Homer walked more than ever like a badly made automaton and his features were set in a rigid, mechanical grin. He had his trousers on over his nightgown and part of it hung out of his open fly. In both of his hands were suitcases. With each step, he lurched to one side then the other, using the suitcases for balance weights.

Tod stopped directly in front of him, blocking his way. "Where're you going?"

"Wayneville," he replied, using an extraordinary amount of jaw movement to get out this single word.

"That's fine. But you can't walk to the station from here. It's in Los Angeles."

Homer tried to get around him, but he caught his arm. "We'll get a taxi. I'll go with you."

The cabs were all being routed around the block because of the preview. He explained this to Homer and tried to get him to walk to the corner.

"Come on, we're sure to get one on the next street."

Once Tod got him into a cab, he intended to tell the driver to go to the nearest hospital. But Homer wouldn't budge, no matter how hard he yanked and pleaded. People stopped to watch them, others turned their heads curiously. He decided to leave him and get a cab.

"I'll come right back," he said.

He couldn't tell from either Homer's eyes or expression whether he heard, for they both were empty of everything, even annoyance. At the corner he looked around and saw that Homer had started to cross the street, moving blindly. Brakes screeched and twice he was almost run over, but he didn't swerve or hurry. He moved in a straight diagonal. When he reached the other curb, he tried to get on the sidewalk at a point where the crowd was very thick and was shoved violently back. He made another attempt and this time a policeman grabbed him by the back of the neck and hustled him to the end of the line. When the policeman let go of him, he kept on walking as though nothing had happened.

Tod tried to get over to him, but was unable to cross until the traffic lights changed. When he reached the other side, he found Homer sitting on a bench, fifty or sixty feet from the outskirts of the crowd.

He put his arm around Homer's shoulder and suggested that they walk a few blocks further. When Homer didn't answer, he reached over to pick up one of the valises. Homer held on to it.

"I'll carry it for you," he said, tugging gently.

"Thief!"

Before Homer could repeat the shout, he jumped away. It would be extremely embarrassing if Homer shouted thief in front of a cop. He thought of phoning for an ambulance. But then, after all, how could he be sure that Homer was crazy? He was sitting quietly on the bench, minding his own business.

Tod decided to wait, then try again to get him into a cab. The crowd was growing in size all the time, but it would be at least half an hour before it over-ran the bench. Before that happened, he would think of some plan. He moved a short distance away and stood with his back to a store window so that he could watch Homer without attracting attention.

About ten feet from where Homer was sitting grew a large eucalyptus tree and behind the trunk of the tree was a little boy. Tod saw him peer around it with great caution, then suddenly jerk his head back. A minute later he repeated the maneuver. At first Tod thought he was playing hide and seek, then noticed that he had a string in his hand which was attached to an old purse that lay in front of Homer's bench. Every once in a while the child would jerk the string, making the purse hop like a sluggish toad. Its torn lining hung from its iron mouth like a furry tongue and a few uncertain flies hovered over it.

Tod knew the game the child was playing. He used to play it himself when he was small. If Homer reached to pick up the purse, thinking there was money in it, he would yank it away and scream with laughter.

When Tod went over to the tree, he was surprised to discover that it was Adore Loomis, the kid who lived across the street from Homer. Tod tried to chase him, but he dodged around the tree, thumbing his nose. He gave up and went back to his original position. The moment he left, Adore got busy with his purse again. Homer wasn't paying any attention to the child, so Tod decided to let him alone.

Mrs. Loomis must be somewhere in the crowd, he thought. Tonight when she found Adore, she would give him a hiding. He had torn the pocket of his jacket and his Buster Brown collar was smeared with grease.

Adore had a nasty temper. The completeness with which

Homer ignored both him and his pocketbook made him frantic. He gave up dancing it at the end of the string and approached the bench on tiptoes, making ferocious faces, yet ready to run at Homer's first move. He stopped when about four feet away and stuck his tongue out. Homer ignored him. He took another step forward and ran through a series of insulting gestures.

If Tod had known that the boy held a stone in his hand, he would have interfered. But he felt sure that Homer wouldn't hurt the child and was waiting to see if he wouldn't move because of his pestering. When Adore raised his arm, it was too late. The stone hit Homer in the face. The boy turned to flee, but tripped and fell. Before he could scramble away, Homer landed on his back with both feet, then jumped again.

Tod yelled for him to stop and tried to yank him away. He shoved Tod and went on using his heels. Tod hit him as hard as he could, first in the belly, then in the face. He ignored the blows and continued to stamp on the boy. Tod hit him again and again, then threw both arms around him and tried to pull him off. He couldn't budge him. He was like a stone column.

The next thing Tod knew, he was torn loose from Homer and sent to his knees by a blow in the back of the head that spun him sideways. The crowd in front of the theatre had charged. He was surrounded by churning legs and feet. He pulled himself erect by grabbing a man's coat, then let himself be carried along backwards in a long, curving swoop. He saw Homer rise above the mass for a moment, shoved against the sky, his jaw hanging as though he wanted to scream but couldn't. A hand reached up and caught him by his open mouth and pulled him forward and down.

There was another dizzy rush. Tod closed his eyes and fought to keep upright. He was jostled about in a hacking cross surf of shoulders and backs, carried rapidly in one direction and then in the opposite. He kept pushing and hitting out at the people around him, trying to face in the direction he was going. Being carried backwards terrified him.

Using the eucalyptus tree as a landmark, he tried to work toward it by slipping sideways against the tide, pushing hard when carried away from it and riding the current when it moved toward his objective. He was within only a few feet of the tree when a sudden, driving rush carried him far past it. He struggled desperately for a moment, then gave up and let himself be swept along. He was the spearhead of a flying wedge when it collided with a mass going in the opposite direction. The impact turned him around. As the two forces ground against each other, he was turned again and again, like a grain between millstones. This didn't stop until he became part of the opposing force. The pressure continued to increase until he thought he must collapse. He was slowly being pushed into the air. Although relief for his cracking ribs could be gotten by continuing to rise, he fought to keep his feet on the ground. Not being able to touch was an even more dreadful sensation than being carried backwards.

There was another rush, shorter this time, and he found himself in a dead spot where the pressure was less and equal. He became conscious of a terrible pain in his left leg, just above the ankle, and tried to work it into a more comfortable position. He couldn't turn his body, but managed to get his head around. A very skinny boy, wearing a Western Union cap, had his back wedged against his shoulder. The pain continued to grow and his whole leg as high as the groin throbbed. He finally got his left arm free and took the back of the boy's neck in his fingers. He twisted as hard as he could. The boy began to jump up and down in his clothes. He managed to straighten his elbow, by pushing at the back of the boy's head, and so turn half-way around and free his leg. The pain didn't grow less.

There was another wild surge forward that ended in another dead spot. He now faced a young girl who was sobbing steadily. Her silk print dress had been torn down the front and her tiny brassiere hung from one strap. He tried by pressing back to give her room, but she moved with him every time he moved. Now and then, she would jerk violently and he wondered if she was going to have a fit. One of her thighs was between his legs. He struggled to get free of her, but she clung to him, moving with him and pressing against him.

She turned her head and said, "Stop, stop," to someone behind her.

He saw what the trouble was. An old man, wearing a Panama hat and horn-rimmed glasses, was hugging her. He had one of his hands inside her dress and was biting her neck.

Tod freed his right arm with a heave, reached over the girl and brought his fist down on the man's head. He couldn't hit very hard but managed to knock the man's hat off, also his glasses. The man tried to bury his face in the girl's shoulder, but Tod grabbed one of his ears and yanked. They started to move again. Tod held on to the ear as long as he could hoping that it would come away in his hand. The girl managed to twist under his arm. A piece of her dress tore, but she was free of her attacker.

Another spasm passed through the mob and he was carried toward the curb. He fought toward a lamp-post, but he was swept by before he could grasp it. He saw another man catch the girl with the torn dress. She screamed for help. He tried to get to her, but was carried in the opposite direction. This rush also ended in a dead spot. Here his neighbors were all shorter than he was. He turned his head upward toward the sky and tried to pull some fresh air into his aching lungs, but it was all heavily tainted with sweat.

In this part of the mob no one was hysterical. In fact, most of the people seemed to be enjoying themselves. Near him was a stout woman with a man pressing hard against her from in front. His chin was on her shoulder, and his arms were around her. She paid no attention to him and went on talking to the woman at her side.

"The first thing I knew," Tod heard her say, "there was a rush and I was in the middle."

"Yeah. Somebody hollered, 'Here comes Gary Cooper,' and then wham!"

"That ain't it," said a little man wearing a cloth cap and pullover sweater. "This is a riot you're in."

"Yeah," said a third woman, whose snaky gray hair was hanging over her face and shoulders. "A pervert attacked a child."

"He ought to be lynched."

Everybody agreed vehemently.

"I come from St. Louis," announced the stout woman, "and we had one of them pervert fellers in our neighborhood once. He ripped up a girl with a pair of scissors."

"He must have been crazy," said the man in the cap. "What kind of fun is that?"

Everybody laughed. The stout woman spoke to the man who was hugging her.

"Hey, you," she said. "I ain't no pillow."

The man smiled beatifically but didn't move. She laughed, making no effort to get out of his embrace.

"A fresh guy," she said.

The other woman laughed.

"Yeah," she said, "this is a regular free-for-all."

The man in the cap and sweater thought there was another laugh in his comment about the pervert.

"Ripping up a girl with scissors. That's the wrong tool."

He was right. They laughed even louder than the first time.

"You'd a done it different, eh, kid?" said a young man with a kidney-shaped head and waxed mustaches.

The two women laughed. This encouraged the man in the cap and he reached over and pinched the stout woman's friend. She squealed.

"Lay off that," she said good-naturedly.

"I was shoved," he said.

An ambulance siren screamed in the street. Its wailing moan started the crowd moving again and Tod was carried along in a slow, steady push. He closed his eyes and tried to protect his throbbing leg. This time, when the movement ended, he found himself with his back to the theatre wall. He kept his eyes closed and stood on his good leg. After what seemed like hours, the pack began to loosen and move again with a churning motion. It gathered momentum and rushed. He rode it until he was slammed against the base of an iron rail which fenced the driveway of the theatre from the street. He had the wind knocked out of him by the impact, but managed to cling to the rail. He held on desperately, fighting to keep from being sucked back. A woman caught him around the waist and tried to hang on. She was sobbing rhythmically. Tod felt his fingers slipping from the rail and kicked backwards as hard as he could. The woman let go.

Despite the agony in his leg, he was able to think clearly about his picture, "The Burning of Los Angeles." After his quarrel with Faye, he had worked on it continually to escape tormenting himself, and the way to it in his mind had become almost automatic.

As he stood on his good leg, clinging desperately to the iron rail, he could see all the rough charcoal strokes with which he had blocked it out on the big canvas. Across the top, parallel with the frame, he had drawn the burning city, a great bonfire of architectural styles, ranging from Egyptian to Cape Cod colonial. Through the center, winding from left to right, was a long hill street and down it, spilling into the middle foreground, came the mob carrying baseball bats and torches. For the faces of its members, he was using the innumerable sketches he had made of the people who come to California to die; the cultists of all sorts, economic as well as religious, the wave, airplane, funeral and preview watchers—all those poor devils who can only be stirred by the promise of miracles and then only to violence. A super "Dr. Know-All Pierce-All" had made the necessary promise and they were marching behind his banner in a great united front of screwballs and screwboxes to purify the land. No longer bored, they sang and danced joyously in the red light of the flames.

In the lower foreground, men and women fled wildly before the vanguard of the crusading mob. Among them were Faye, Harry, Homer, Claude and himself. Faye ran proudly, throwing her knees high. Harry stumbled along behind her, holding on to his beloved derby hat with both hands. Homer seemed to be falling out of the canvas, his face half-asleep, his big hands clawing the air in anguished pantomime. Claude turned his head as he ran to thumb his nose at his pursuers. Tod himself picked up a small stone to throw before continuing his flight.

He had almost forgotten both his leg and his predicament, and to make his escape still more complete he stood on a chair and worked at the flames in an upper corner of the canvas, modeling the tongues of fire so that they licked even more avidly at a corinthian column that held up the palmleaf roof of a nutburger stand.

He had finished one flame and was starting on another when he was brought back by someone shouting in his ear. He opened his eyes and saw a policeman trying to reach him from behind the rail to which he was clinging. He let go with his left hand and raised his arm. The policeman caught him by the wrist, but couldn't lift him. Tod was afraid to let go until another man came to aid the policeman and caught him by the back of his jacket. He let go of the rail and they hauled him up and over it.

When they saw that he couldn't stand, they let him down easily to the ground. He was in the theatre driveway. On the curb next to him sat a woman crying into her skirt. Along the wall were groups of other disheveled people. At the end of the driveway was an ambulance. A policeman asked him if he wanted to go to the hospital. He shook his head no. He then offered him a lift home. Tod had the presence of mind to give Claude's address.

He was carried through the exit to the back street and lifted into a police car. The siren began to scream and at first he thought he was making the noise himself. He felt his lips with his hands. They were clamped tight. He knew then it was the siren. For some reason this made him laugh and he began to imitate the siren as loud as he could.

The Dream Life of Balso Snell

TO A. S.

*"After all, my dear fellow,
life, Anaxagoras has said,
is a journey."*

BERGOTTE

1

While walking in the tall grass that has sprung up around the city of Troy, Balso Snell came upon the famous wooden horse of the Greeks. A poet, he remembered Homer's ancient song and decided to find a way in.

On examining the horse, Balso found that there were but three openings: the mouth, the navel, and the posterior opening of the alimentary canal. The mouth was beyond his reach, the navel proved a cul-de-sac, and so, forgetting his dignity, he approached the last. O Anus Mirabilis!

Along the lips of the mystic portal he discovered writings which after a little study he was able to decipher. Engraved in a heart pierced by an arrow and surmounted by the initial N, he read, "Ah! Qualis . . . Artifex . . . Pereo!" Not to be outdone by the actor-emperor, Balso carved with his penknife another heart and the words "O Byss! O Abyss! O Anon! O Anan!" omitting, however, the arrow and his initial.

Before entering he prayed:

"O Beer! O Meyerbeer! O Bach! O Offenbach! Stand me now as ever in good stead."

Balso immediately felt like the One at the Bridge, the Two in the Bed, the Three in the Boat, the Four on Horseback, the Seven Against Thebes. And with a high heart he entered the gloom of the foyer-like lower intestine.

After a little while, seeing no one and hearing nothing, Balso began to feel depressed. To keep his heart high and yet out of his throat, he made a song.

Round as the Anus
Of a Bronze Horse
Or the Tender Buttons
Used by Horses for Ani

On the Wheels of His Car
Ringed Round with Brass
Clamour the Seraphim
Tongues of Our Lord

Full Ringing Round
As the Belly of Silenus
Giotto Painter of Perfect Circles
Goes . . . One Motion Round

Round and Full
Round and Full as

A Brimming Goblet
The Dew-Loaded Navel
Of Mary
Of Mary Our Mother

Round and Ringing Full
As the Mouth of a Brimming Goblet
The Rust-Laden Holes
In Our Lord's Feet.
Entertain the Jew-Driven Nails.

He later gave this song various names, the most successful of which were: *Anywhere Out of the World, or a Voy-
age Through the Hole in the Mundane Millstone* and At
*Hoops with the Ani of Bronze Horses, or Toe Holes for a
Flight of Fancy.*

But despite the gaiety of his song, Balso did not feel sure
of himself. He thought of the Phoenix Excrementi, a race of
men he had invented one Sunday afternoon while in bed,
and trembled, thinking he might well meet one in this
place. And he had good cause to tremble, for the Phoenix
Excrementi eat themselves, digest themselves, and give
birth to themselves by evacuating their bowels.

Hoping to attract the attention of an inhabitant, Balso
shouted as though overwhelmed by the magnificence of his
surroundings:

"O the Rose Gate! O the Moist Garden! O Well! O Fountain! O Sticky Flower! O Mucous Membrane!"

A man with "Tours" embroidered on his cap stalked out
of the shadow. In order to prove a poet's right to trespass,
Balso quoted from his own works:

"If you desire to have two parallel lines meet at once or
even in the near future," he said, "it is important to make
all the necessary arrangements beforehand, preferably by
wireless."

The man ignored his little speech. "Sir," he said, "you are

an ambassador from that ingenious people, the inventors and perfectors of the automatic water-closet, to my people who are the heirs of Greece and Rome. As your own poet has so well put it, 'The Grandeur that was Greece and the Glory that was Rome' . . . I offer you my services as guide. First you will please look to the right where you will see a beautiful Doric prostate gland swollen with gladness and an over-abundance of good cheer."

This speech made Balso very angry. "Inventors of the automatic water-closet, are we?" he shouted. "Oh, you stinker! Doric, bah! It's Baptist '68, that's what it is. And no prostate gland either, simply an atrophied pile. You call this dump grand and glorious, do you? Have you ever seen the Grand Central Station, or the Yale Bowl, or the Holland Tunnel, or the New Madison Square Garden? Exposed plumbing, stinker, that's all I see—and at this late date. It's criminally backward, do you hear me?"

The guide gave ground before Balso's rage. "Please sir," he said, "please . . . After all, the ages have sanctified this ground, great men have hallowed it. In Rome do as the Romans do."

"Stinker," Balso repeated, but less ferociously this time.

The guide took heart. "Mind your manners, foreigner. If you don't like it here, why don't you go back where you came from? But before you go let me tell you a story—an old tale of my people, rich in local color. And, you force me to say it, apropos, timely. However, let me assure you that I mean no offense. The title of the story is

"VISITORS

"A traveler in Tyana, who was looking for the sage Appolonius, saw a snake enter the lower part of a man's body. Approaching the man, he said:

" 'Pardon me, my good fellow, but a snake just entered your . . .' He finished by pointing.

" 'Yes sir, he lives there,' was the astounding rejoinder.

" 'Ah, then you must be the man I'm looking for, the philosopher-saint, Appolonius of Tyana. Here is a letter of introduction from my brother George. May I see the snake please? Now the opening. Perfect!' "

Balso echoed the last word of the story. "Perfect! Perfect! A real old-world fable. You may consider yourself hired."

"I have other stories to tell," the guide said, "and I shall tell them as we go along. By the way, have you heard the one about Moses and the Burning Bush? How the prophet rebuked the Bush for speaking by quoting the proverb, 'Good wine needs no bush'; and how the Bush insolently replied, 'A hand in the Bush is worth two in the pocket.' "

Balso did not consider this story nearly as good as the other; in fact he thought it very bad, yet he was determined to make no more breaks and entered the large intestine on the arm of his guide. He let the guide do all the talking and they made great headway up the tube. But, unfortunately, coming suddenly upon a place where the intestine had burst through the stomach wall, Balso cried out in amazement:

"What a hernia! What a hernia!"

The guide began to splutter with rage and Balso tried to pacify him by making believe he had not meant the scenery. "Hernia," he said, rolling the word on his tongue. "What a pity childish associations cling to beautiful words such as hernia, making their use as names impossible. Hernia! What a beautiful name for a girl! Hernia Hornstein! Paresis Pearlberg! Paranoia Puntz! How much more pleasing to the ear [and what other sense should a name please?] than Faith Rabinowitz or Hope Hilkowitz."

But Balso had only blundered again. "Sirrah!" the guide cried in an enormous voice, "I am a Jew! and whenever anything Jewish is mentioned, I find it necessary to say that I am a Jew. I'm a Jew! A Jew!"

"Oh, you mistake me," Balso said, "I have nothing against the Jews. I admire the Jews; they are a thrifty race. Some of my best friends are Jews." But his protests availed him little until he thought to quote C. M. Doughty's epigram. "The semites," Balso said with great firmness, "are like to a man sitting in a cloaca to the eyes, and whose brows touch heaven."

When Balso had at last succeeded in quieting the guide, he tried to please him further by saying that the magnificent tunnel stirred him to the quick and that he would be satisfied to spend his remaining days in it with but a few pipes and a book.

The guide tossed up his arms in one of those eloquent gestures the latins know so well how to perform and said:

"After all, what is art? I agree with George Moore. Art is not nature, but rather nature digested. Art is a sublime excrement."

"And Daudet?" Balso queried.

"Oh, Daudet! Daudet, c'est de bouillabaisse! You know, George Moore also says, 'What care I that the virtue of some sixteen-year-old maiden was the price paid for Ingres' La Source?' Now . . ."

"Picasso says," Balso broke in, "Picasso says there are no feet in nature . . . And, thanks for showing me around. I have to leave."

But before he was able to get away, the guide caught him by the collar. "Just a minute, please. You were right to interrupt. We should talk of art, not artists. Please explain your interpretation of the Spanish master's dictum."

"Well, the point is . . ." Balso began. But before he could finish the guide started again. "If you are willing to acknowledge the existence of points," he said, "then the statement that there are no feet in nature puts you in an

untenable position. It depends for its very meaning on the
fact that there are no points. Picasso, by making this asser-
tion, has placed himself on the side of monism in the eternal wrangle between the advocates of the Singular and
those of the Plural. As James puts it, 'Does reality exist
distributively or collectively—in the shape of *eaches,
everys, anys, eithers* or only in the shape of an *all* or *whole?'*
If reality is singular then there are no feet in nature, if
plural, a great many. If the world is one [everything part
of the same thing—called by Picasso nature] then nothing
either begins or ends. Only when things take the shapes of
eaches, everys, anys, eithers [have ends] do they have feet.
Feet are attached to ends, by definition. Moreover, if
everything is one, and has neither ends nor beginnings,
then everything is a circle. A circle has neither a beginning
nor an end. A circle has no feet. If we believe that nature is
a circle, then we must also believe that there are no feet in
nature.

"Do not pooh-pooh this idea as mystical. Bergson
has . . ."

"Cezanne said, 'Everything tends toward the globular.'"
With this announcement Balso made another desperate attempt to escape.

"Cezanne?" the guide said, keeping a firm hold on
Balso's collar. "Cezanne is right. The sage of Aix is . . ."

With a violent twist, Balso tore loose and fled.

Balso fled down the great tunnel until he came upon a
man, naked except for a derby in which thorns were stick-

ing, who was attempting to crucify himself with thumb tacks. His curiosity got the better of his fear and he stopped.

"Can I help you?" he asked politely.

"No," the man answered with even greater politeness, tipping his hat repeatedly as he spoke. "No, I can manage, thank you . . .

"My name is Maloney the Areopagite," the man continued, answering the questions Balso was too well-bred to word, "and I am a catholic mystic. I believe implicitly in that terrible statement of Saint Hildegarde's, 'The lord dwells not in the bodies of the healthy and vigorous.' I live as did Marie Alacoque, Suso, Labre, Lydwine of Schiedam, Rose of Lima. When my suffering is not too severe, I compose verses in imitation of Notker Balbus, Ekkenard le Vieux, Hucbald le Chauve.

"In the feathered darkness
Of thy mouth,
O Mother of God!
I worship Christ
The culminating rose.

"Get the idea? I spend the rest of my time marveling at the love shown by all the great saints for even the lowliest of God's creatures. Have you ever heard of Benedict Labre? It was he who picked up the vermin that fell out of his hat and placed them piously back into his sleeve. Before calling in a laundress, another very holy man removed the vermin from his clothes in order not to drown the jewels of sanctity infesting them.

"Inspired by these thoughts I have decided to write the biography of Saint Puce, a great martyred member of the vermin family. If you are interested, I will give you a short précis of his life.

"Please do so, sir," Balso said. "Live and learn is my motto, Mr. Maloney, so please continue."

"Saint Puce was a flea," Maloney the Areopagite began in a well-trained voice. "A flea who was born, lived, and died, beneath the arm of our Lord.

"Saint Puce was born from an egg that was laid in the flesh of Christ while as a babe He played on the floor of the stable in Bethlehem. That the flesh of a god has been a stage in the incubation of more than one being is well known: Dionysius and Athene come to mind.

"Saint Puce had two mothers: the winged creature that laid the egg, and the God that hatched it in His flesh. Like most of us, he had two fathers: our Father Who art in Heaven, and he who in the cocksureness of our youth we called 'pop.'

"Which of his two fathers fertilized the egg? I cannot answer with certainty, but the subsequent actions of Saint Puce's life lead me to believe that the egg was fertilized by a being whose wings were of feathers. Yes, I mean the Dove or Paraclete—the Sanctus Spiritus. In defense of this belief antiquity will help us again: it is only necessary to remember Leda and Europa. And I must remind you, you who might plead a puce too small physically, of the nature of God's love and how it embraceth all.

"O happy, happy childhood! Playing in the curled brown silk, sheltered from all harm by Christ's arm. Eating the sweet flesh of our Saviour; drinking His blood; bathing in His sweat; partaking, oh how fully! of His Godhead. Having no need to cry as I have cried:

"Corpus Christi, salva me
Sanguis Christi, inebria me
Aqua lateris Christi, lave me.

"In manhood, fullgrown, how strong Saint Puce was, how lusty; and how his lust and strength were satisfied in one continuous, never-culminating ecstasy. The music of our Lord's skin sliding over His flesh!—more exact than the fugues of Bach. The pattern of His veins!—more intricate than the Maze at Cnossos. The odors of His Body!—more fragant than the Temple of Solomon. The temperature of His flesh!—more pleasant than the Roman baths to the youth Puce. And, finally, the taste of His blood! In this wine all pleasure, all excitement, was magnified, until with ecstasy Saint Puce's small body roared like a furnace.

"In his prime, Saint Puce wandered far from his birth-place, that hairsilk pocketbook, the armpit of our Lord. He roamed the forest of God's chest and crossed the hill of His abdomen. He measured and sounded that fathomless well, the Navel of our Lord. He explored and charted every crevasse, ridge, and cavern of Christ's body. From notes taken during his travels he later wrote his great work, A Geography of Our Lord.

"After much wandering, tired, he returned at last to his home in the savoury forest. To spend, he thought, his remaining days in writing, worship, and contemplation. Happy in a church whose walls were the flesh of Christ, whose windows were rose with the blood of Christ, and on whose altars burned golden candles made of the sacred earwax.

"Soon, too soon, alas! the day of martyrdom arrived [O Jesu, mi dulcissime!], and the arms of Christ were lifted that His hands might receive the nails.

"The walls and windows of Saint Puce's church were broken and its halls flooded with blood.

"The hot sun of Calvary burnt the flesh beneath Christ's upturned arm, making the petal-like skin shrivel until it looked like the much-shaven armpit of an old actress.

"After Christ died, Saint Puce died, refusing to desert to lesser flesh, even to that of Mary who stood close under the cross. With his last strength he fought off the unconquerable worm. . . ."

Mr. Maloney's thin frame was racked by sobs as he finished, yet Balso did not spare him.

"I think you're morbid," he said. "Don't be morbid. Take your eyes off your navel. Take your head from under your armpit. Stop sniffing mortality. Play games. Don't read so many books. Take cold showers. Eat more meat."

With these helpful words, Balso left him to his own devices and continued on his way.

He had left Maloney the Areopagite far behind when, on turning a bend in the intestine, he saw a boy hiding what looked like a packet of letters in a hollow tree. After the boy had left, Balso removed the packet and sat down to read. First, however, he took off his shoes because his feet hurt.

What he had taken for letters proved on closer scrutiny to be a diary. At the top of the first page was written, "English Theme by John Gilson, Class 8B, Public School 186, Miss McGeeney, teacher." He read further.

Jan. 1st—at home

Whom do I fool by calling these pages a journal? Surely not you, Miss McGeeney. Alas! no-one. Nor is anyone fooled by the fact that I write in the first person. It is for this reason that I do not claim to have found these pages in a hollow tree. I am an honest man and feel badly about masks, cardboard noses, diaries, memoirs, letters from a Sabine farm, the theatre . . . I feel badly, yet I can do nothing. 'Sir!' I say to myself, 'your name is not Iago, but simply John. It is monstrous to write lies in a diary.'

However, I insist that I am an honest man. Reality troubles me as it must all honest men.

Reality! Reality! If I could only discover the Real. A Real that I could know with my senses. A Real that would wait for me to inspect it as a dog inspects a dead rabbit. But, alas! when searching for the Real I throw a stone into a pool whose ripples become of advancing less importance until they are too large for connection with, or even memory of, the stone agent.

Written while smelling the moistened forefinger of my left hand.

Jan 2nd—at home

Is this journal to be like all the others I have started? A large first entry, consisting of the incident which made me think my life exciting enough to keep a journal, followed by a series of entries gradually decreasing in size and culminating in a week of blank days.

Inexperienced diary-writers make their first entry the largest. They come to the paper with a constipation of ideas—eager, impatient. The white paper acts as a laxative. A diarrhoea of words is the result. The richness of the flow is unnatural; it cannot be sustained.

A diary must grow naturally—a flower, a cancer, a civilization . . . In a diary there is no need for figures of speech, honest Iago.

Sometimes my name is Raskolnikov, sometimes it is Iago. I never was, and never shall be, plain John Gilson—honest, honest Iago, yes, but never honest John. As Raskolnikov, I keep a journal which I call *The Making of a Fiend*. I give the heart of my Crime Journal:

Crime Journal

I have been in this hospital seven weeks. I am under observation. Am I sane? This diary shall prove me insane.

This entry gives me away.

Crime Journal

My mother visited me today. She cried. It is she who is crazy. Order is the test of sanity. Her emotions and thoughts are disordered. Mine are arranged, valued, placed.

Man spends a great deal of time making order out of chaos, yet insists that the emotions be disordered. I order my emotions: I am insane. Yet sanity is discipline. My mother rolls on the hospital floor and cries: "John darling . . . John sweetheart." Her hat falls over face. She clutches her absurd bag of oranges. She is sane.

I say to her quietly: "Mother, I love you, but this spectacle is preposterous—and the smell of your clothing depresses me." I am insane.

Crime Journal

Order is vanity. I have decided to discard the nonsense of precision instruments. No more measuring. I drop the slide rule and take up the Golden Rule. Sanity is the absence of extremes.

Crime Journal

Is someone reading my diary while I sleep?

On reading what I have written, I think I can detect a peculiar change in my words. They have taken on the quality of comment.

You who read these pages while I sleep, please sign your name here.

John Raskolnikov Gilson

Crime Journal

During the night I got up, turned to yesterday's entry and signed my name.

Crime Journal

I am insane. I [the papers had it CULTURED FIEND SLAYS DISHWASHER] am insane.

When a baby, I affected all the customary poses: I "laughed the icy laughter of the soul," I uttered "universal sighs"; I sang in "silver-fire verse"; I smiled the "enigmatic smile"; I sought "azure and elliptical routes." In everything I was completely the mad poet. I was one of those "great despisers," whom Nietzche loved because "they are the great adorers; they are arrows of longing for the other shore." Along with "mon hysterie" I cultivated a "rotten, ripe maturity." You understand what I mean: like Rimbaud, I practiced having hallucinations.

Now, my imagination is a wild beast that cries always for freedom. I am continually tormented by the desire to indulge some strange thing, perceptible but indistinct, hidden in the swamps of my mind. This hidden thing is always crying out to me from its hiding-place: "Do as I tell you and you will find out my shape. There, quick! what is that thing in your brain? Indulge my commands and some day the great doors of your mind will swing open and allow you to enter and handle to your complete satisfaction the vague shapes and figures hidden there."

I can know nothing; I can have nothing; I must devote my whole life to the pursuit of a shadow. It is as if I were attempting to trace with the point of a pencil the shadow of the tracing pencil. I am enchanted with the shadow's shape and want very much to outline it; but the shadow is attached to the pencil and moves with it, never allowing me to trace its tempting form. Because of some great need, I am continually forced to make the attempt.

Two years ago I sorted books for eight hours a day in the public library. Can you imagine how it feels to be surrounded for eight long hours by books—a hundred billion words one after another according to ten thousand mad schemes. What patience, what labor are those crazy sequences the result of! What starving! What sacrifice! And the fervors, deliriums, ambitions, dreams, that dictated them! . . .

The books smelt like the breaths of their authors; the books smelt like a closet full of old shoes through which a steam pipe passes. As I handled them they seemed to turn into flesh, or at lest some substance that could be eaten.

Have you ever spent any time among the people who farm the great libraries: the people who search old issues of the medical journals for pornography and facts about strange diseases; the comic writers who exhume jokes from old magazines; the men and women employed by the insurance companies to gather statistics on death? I worked in the philosophy department. That department is patronized by alchemists, astrologers, cabalists, demonologists, magicians, atheists, and the founders of new religious systems.

While working in the library, I lived in a theatrical rooming house in the west Forties, a miserable, uncomfortable place. I lived there because of the discomfort. I wanted to be miserable. I could not have lived in a comfortable house. The noises [harsh, grating], the dirt [animal, greasy], the smells [dry sweat, sour mold], permitted me to wallow in my discomfort. My mind was full of vague irritations and annoyances. My body was nervous and jumpy, and demanded an extraordinary amount of sleep. I was a bundle of physical and mental tics. I climbed into myself like a bear into a hollow tree, and lay there long hours, overpowered by the heat, odor, and nastiness of I.

The only other person living on my floor, the top one,

was an idiot. He earned his living as a dishwasher in the kitchen of the Hotel Astor. He was a fat, pink and grey pig of a man, and stank of stale tobacco, dry perspiration, clothing mold, and oatmeal soap. He did not have a skull on the top of his neck, only a face; his head was all face—a face without side, back or top, like a mask.

The idiot never wore a collar, yet he kept both a front and a back collar button in the neckband of his shirt. When he changed his shirt he removed the collar buttons from the dirty shirt and placed them in the clean one. His neck was smooth, white, fat, and covered all over with tiny blue veins like a piece of cheap marble. His Adam's apple was very large and looked as though it might be a soft tumor in his throat. When he swallowed, his neck bulged out and he made a sound like a miniature toilet being flushed.

My neighbor, the idiot, never smiled, but laughed continually. It must have hurt him to laugh. He fought his laughter as though it were a wild beast. A beast of laughter seemed always struggling to escape from between his teeth.

People say that it is terrible to hear a man cry. I think it is even worse to hear a man laugh. [Yet the ancients considered hysteria a woman's disease. They believed that hysteria was caused by the womb breaking loose and floating freely through the body. The cure they practiced was to place sweet-smelling herbs to the vulva in order to attract the womb back to its original position, and foul-smelling things to the nose in order to keep the womb away from the head.]

One night at the movies, I heard a basso from the Chicago Opera Company sing the devil's serenade from Faust. A portion of this song calls for a long laugh. When the singer came to the laugh he was unable to get started. He struggled with the laugh, but it refused to come. At last he managed to start laughing. Once started, he was unable to stop. The orchestra repeated the transition that led from the laugh to the next bars of the song, but he was unable to stop laughing.

I returned home with my head full of the singer's laughter. Because of it I was unable to fall asleep. I dressed myself and went downstairs. On my way to the street I passed my neighbor the idiot. He was laughing to himself. His laughter made me laugh. When he detected the strain in my voice he grew angry. He thought that I was making fun of him. He said, "Who you laughing at?" I became frightened and offered him a cigarette. He refused it. I left him on the stairs, struggling with his laughter and his anger.

I knew that if I did not get my customary amount of sleep, I would suffer when the time came for me to get up. I was certain that if I went back to bed I would be unable to sleep. In order to tire myself as quickly as possible, I walked to Broadway and then started uptown. My shoes hurt me and at first I enjoyed the pain. Soon, however, the pain became so intense that I had to stop walking and return home.

On regaining my bed, I still found it impossible to fall asleep. I knew that I must become interested in something outside of myself or go insane. I plotted the death of the idiot.

I felt certain that it would be a safe murder to commit. Safe, because its motives would not be comprehensible to the police. Policemen are reasonable men; they do not consider the shape and color of a man's throat, his laugh or the fact that he does not wear a collar, reasonable motives for killing him.

You also, eh, doctor, consider these poor reasons for murder. I agree—they are literary reasons. Reasoning your way, dear doctor—like Darwin or a policeman—I am expected to trace my action back to some such things as the desire to live or create life. Because I want you to believe me, I shall say that in order to remain sane I had to kill this man, just as I had to kill, when a child, all the flies in my room before being able to fall asleep.

Nonsense, eh? I agree—nonsense. Please, please—here [please believe me] is why I killed Adolph. I killed the idiot because he disturbed my sense of balance. I killed him thinking his death would permit me to regain my balance. My beloved balance!

The fact that I had never killed made me uncomfortable. What was this enormous crime I had never committed? What were all the horrors attendant on this act? I killed a man and discovered the answers. I shall never kill another man. I shall never need to kill another man.

Let me continue with my confession. I decided not to plot an intricate killing. I was afraid that if I attempted a complicated crime I might get entangled in my own scheme. I decided to have the murder consist of only one act, the killing. I even resisted the desire to look up certain books in the library.

Because the idea of the killing involved the dishwasher's throat, I decided to do the job with a knife. As a child I always took pleasure in cutting soft, firm things. I purchased a knife about fifteen inches long. The knife had only one cutting edge; the other edge or the back of the knife was about half an inch thick. Its weight made it a perfect instrument for the job.

I did not want to commit the murder too soon after purchasing the knife; but on the very night that I brought it home, I heard the idiot come up the stairs drunk. As I listened to him fumble with his key, I realized, for the first time, that he locked his door at night. This unlooked-for obstacle almost made me give up the idea of killing him. I rid myself of my misgivings by thinking of the torture I would have to go through if I frustrated my desire to commit murder. I decided to do the job that very evening and have it over with. I put on my bathrobe and went into the hall. His door was ajar. I went to it carefully. The idiot was stretched out on his bed, drunk. I went back to my room and took off my bathrobe and pajamas. I planned to do the murder naked, so that I should have no blood-stained things to wash or destroy. What blood I got on my body I could easily wash off. Naked: I felt cold; and I noticed that my genitals were tight and hard, like a dog's, or an archaic Greek statue's—they were as though I had just come out of an ice-cold bath. I was aware of a great excitement; an excitement that seemed to be near, but not quite within me.

I crossed the hall and entered the dishwasher's room. He had left his light burning. I walked to him and cut his throat. I had intended to do the cutting with several rapid strokes, but he awoke at the touch of the steel and I became frightened and sawed at his throat in a panic. When he lay still I calmed down.

I went back to my room and stood the knife up in the sink, like one does a wet umbrella, letting what blood was on it run into the drain. I dressed quickly, obsessed by the need for getting rid of the knife. While dressing I became conscious of a growing fear. A fear that as it grew seemed likely to burst me open; a fear so large that I felt I could not contain it without rupturing my mind. Inside of my head this expanding fear was like a rapidly growing child inside the belly of a mother. I felt that I must get rid of the fear or burst. I opened my mouth wide, but I was unable to give birth to my fear.

Carrying this fear as an ant carries a caterpiller thirty times its size, I ran down the stairs and into the street. I hurried west toward the river.

I let the knife slip into the water. With the knife went my fear. I felt light and free. I felt like a happy girl. I said to myself: "You feel like a young girl—kittenish, cuneycutey, darlingey, springtimey." I caressed my breasts like a young girl who has suddenly become conscious of her body on a hot afternoon. I imitated the mannered walk of a girl showing off before a group of boys. In the dark I hugged myself.

On my way back to Broadway I passed some sailors, and felt an overwhelming desire to flirt with them. I went through all the postures of a desperate prostitute; I camped for all I was worth. The sailors looked at me and laughed. I wanted very much for one of them to follow me. Suddenly I heard the sound of footsteps behind me. The steps came close and I felt as though I were melting—all silk and perfumed, pink lace. I died the little death. But the man went past without noticing me. I sat down on a bench and was violently sick.

I sat on the bench for a long time, and then returned to my room, sick and cold.

Inside of my head the murder has become like a piece of sand inside the shell of an oyster. My mind has commenced to form a pearl around it. The idiot, the singer, his laugh, the knife, the river, my change of sex, all cover the murder just as the secretions of an oyster cover an irritating grain of sand. As the accumulations grow and become solidified, the original irritation disappears. If the murder continues to grow in size it may become too large for me to contain; then I am afraid it will kill me, just as the pearl eventually kills the oyster.

Balso put the manuscript back into the tree and continued on his way, his head bowed in thought. The world was get·

ting to be a difficult place for a lyric poet. He felt old. "Ah youth!" he sighed elaborately. "Ah Balso Snell!"

Suddenly he heard a voice at his elbow.

"Well, nosey, how did you like my theme?"

Balso turned and saw the boy whose diary he had been reading. He was still in short pants and looked less than twelve years old.

"Interesting psychologically, but is it art?" Balso said timidly. "I'd give you B minus and a good spanking."

"What the hell do I care about art! Do you know why I wrote that ridiculous story—because Miss McGeeney, my English teacher, reads Russian novels and I want to sleep with her. But maybe you run a magazine. Will you buy it? I need money."

"No, son, I'm a poet. I'm Balso Snell, the poet."

"A poet! For Christ's sake!"

"What you ought to do, child, is to run about more. Read less and play baseball."

"Forget it. I know a fat girl who only sleeps with poets. When I'm with her I'm a poet, too. I won her with a poem.

"O Beast of Walls!
O Walled-in Fat Girl!
Your conquest was hardly worth
The while of one whom Arras and
Arrat, Pelion, Ossa, Parnassus, Ida,
Pisgah and Pike's Peak never in-
terested.

"Not bad, eh? But I'm fed up with poetry and art. Yet what can I do. I need women and because I can't buy or force them, I have to make poems for them. God knows how tired I am of using the insanity of Van Gogh and the adventures of Gauguin as can-openers for the ambitious Count Six-Times. And how sick I am of literary bitches. But they're the only kind that'll have me. . . . Listen, Balso, for a dollar I'll sell you a brief outline of my position."

Balso gave the dollar to get rid of him and received in return a little pamphlet.

THE PAMPHLET

Yesterday, while debating whether I should shave or not, news of the death of my friend Saniette arrived. I decided not to shave.

Today, while shaving, I searched myself for yesterday's emotions. Searched, that is, the pockets of my dressing gown and the shelves of the medicine closet. Not finding anything, I looked further. I looked [first smiling, of course] into the bowels of my compassion, the depths of my being, and even into the receding vistas of my memory. I came from my search, as was to be expected, empty-handed. My "Open, oh flood gates of feeling! Empty, oh vials of passion!" made certain and immediate the defeat of my purpose.

That I failed in my search was for me a sign of my intelligence. I am [just as children choose sides to play "cops and robbers" or "Indians and cowboys"] on the side of intellect against the emotions, on the side of the brain against the heart. Nevertheless, I recognized the cardboard and tin of my position [a young man, while shaving, dismisses Death with a wave of his hand] and did not give up my search for an emotion. I marshalled all my reasons for grief [I had lived with Saniette for almost two years], yet failed to find sorrow.

Death is a very difficult thing for me to consider sincerely because I find certain precomposed judgments awaiting my method of consideration to render it absurd. No matter how I form my comment I attach to it the criticisms sentimental, satirical, formal. With these judgments there goes a series of literary associations which remove me still further from genuine feeling. The very act of recognizing Death, Love, Beauty—all the major subjects—has become, from literature and exercise, impossible.

After admitting to myself that I had failed, I tried to cover my defeat by practicing a few sneers in the bathroom mirror. I remembered that yesterday I had used Saniette's death as an excuse for not shaving and added in a loud voice, "Just as more than one friend will use the occasion of my death as an excuse for breaking an undesired appointment."

Heartened by my sneering reflection in the mirror, I pictured the death of Saniette. Hiding under the blankets of her hospital bed and invoking the aid of Mother Eddy and Doctor Coué: "I won't die! I am getting better and better. I won't die! The will is master o'er the flesh. I won't die!" Only to have Death answer: "Oh, yes you will." And she had. I made Death's triumph my own.

The inevitability of death has always given me pleasure, not because I am eager to die, but because all the Saniettes must die. When the preacher explained the one thing all men could be certain of—all must die—the King of France became angry. When death prevailed over the optimism of Saniette, she was, I am certain, surprised. The thought of Saniette's surprise pleases me, just as the King's anger must have pleased the preacher.

Only a portion of my dislike for Saniette is based on the natural antipathy pessimists feel for optimists, cowboys for Indians, cops for robbers. For a large part it consists of that equally natural antipathy felt by the performer for his audience. My relations with Saniette were exactly those of performer and audience.

While living with me, Saniette accepted my most desperate feats in somewhat the manner one watches the marvelous stunts of acrobats. Her casualness excited me so that I became more and more desperate in my performances. A tragedy with only one death is nothing in the theatre—why not two deaths? Why not a hundred? With some such idea as this in mind I exhibited my innermost organs: I wore my heart and genitals around my neck. At each exhibition I watched carefully to see how she received my performance—with a smile or with a tear. Though I exhibited myself as a clown, I wanted no mistakes to be made; I was a tragic clown.

I have forgotten the time when I could look back at an affair with a woman and remember anything but a sequence of theatrical poses—poses that I assumed, no matter how aware I was of their ridiculousness, because they were amusing. All my acting has but one purpose, the attraction of the female.

If it had been possible for me to attract by exhibiting a series of physical charms, my hatred would have been less. But I found it necessary to substitute strange conceits, wise and witty sayings, peculiar conduct, Art, for the muscles, teeth, hair, of my rivals.

All this much-exhibited intelligence is but a development of the instinct to please. My case is similar to that of a bird called the Amblyornis inornata. As his name indicates, the Inornata is a dull-colored, ugly bird. Yet the Inornata is cousin to the Bird of Paradise. Because he lacks his cousin's brilliant plumage, he has to exteriorize internal feathers. The Inornata plants a garden and builds a house of flowers as a substitute for the gay feathers of his relative. Of course the female Inornata loves her shabby artist dearly; yet when a friend passes, Mrs. Bird of Paradise can say, "Show your tail, dear," while Mrs. Inornata, to her confusion, has no explanation to give for her love. If she is in a temper she might even ask Mr. Inornata to exteriorize a few internal feathers. Still more, the Bird of

Paradise cannot be blamed for the quality of his tail—it just grew. The Inornata, however, is held personally responsible for his performance as an artist.

There was a time when I felt that I was indeed a rare spirit. Then I had genuinely expressed my personality with a babe's delight in confessing the details of its inner life. Soon, however, in order to interest my listeners, I found it necessary to shorten my long outpourings; to make them, by straining my imagination, spectacular. Oh, how much work goes into the search for the odd, the escape from the same!

Because of women like Saniette, I acquired the habit of extravagant thought. I now convert everything into fantastic entertainment and the extraordinary has become an obsession. . . .

An intelligent man finds it easy to laugh at himself, but his laughter is not sincere if it is thorough. If I could be Hamlet, or even a clown with a breaking heart 'neath his jester's motley, the role would be tolerable. But I always find it necessary to burlesque the mystery of feeling at its source; I must laugh at myself, and if the laugh is "bitter," I must laugh at the laugh. The ritual of feeling demands burlesque and, whether the burlesque is successful or not, a laugh. . . .

One night, while in a hotel bedroom with Saniette, I grew miserably sick of the mad dreams I had been describing to amuse her. I began to beat her. While beating her, I was unable to forget that strange man, John Raskolnikov Gilson, the Russian student. As I beat her, I shouted: "O constipation of desire! O diarrhoea of love! O life within life! O mystery of being! O Young Women's Christian Association! Oh! Oh!"

When her screams brought the hotel clerk to our door,

I attempted to explain my irritation. In part I said: "This evening I am very nervous. I have a sty on my eye, a cold sore on my lip, a pimple where the edge of my collar touches my neck, another pimple in the corner of my mouth, and a drop of salt snot on the end of my nose. Because I rub them continually my nostrils are inflamed, sore and angry.

"My forehead is wrinkled so hard that it hurts, yet I cannot unwrinkle it. I spend many hours trying to unwrinkle my forehead. I try to catch myself by surprise; I try to smooth my forehead with my fingers; I try to concentrate my whole mind to this end, but I am unable to make smooth my brow. The skin over my eyebrows is tied in an aching, unbreakable knot.

"The wood of this table, the glasses on it, this girl's woollen dress, the skin under it, excites and annoys me. It seems to me as though all the materials of life—wood, glass, wool, skin—are rubbing against my sty, my cold sore and my pimples; rubbing in such a way as not to satisfy the itch or convert irritation into active pain, but so as to increase the size of the irritation, magnify it and make it seem to cover everything—hysteria, despair.

"I go to a mirror and squeeze the sty with all my strength. I tear off the cold sore with my nails. I scrub my salt-encrusted nostrils with the rough sleeve of my overcoat. If I could only turn irritation into pain; could push the whole thing into insanity and so escape. I am able to turn irritation into active pain for only a few seconds, but the pain soon subsides and the monotonous rhythm of irritation returns. O how fleeting is pain!—I cry. I think of sandpapering my body. I think of grease, of sandalwood oil, of saliva; I think of velvet, of Keats, of music, of the hardness of precious stones, of mathematics, of the arrangements of architecture. But, alas! I can find no relief."

Both Saniette and the clerk refused to understand. Saniette said that she understood the irritation I was talking about was one of the spirit; yet, she added, the only conclusion she could arrive at—a gentleman would never strike a lady—was that I no longer loved her. The clerk murmured something about the police.

In order to get him away from the door, I asked him if he had ever heard of the Marquis de Sade or of Gilles de Rais. Fortunately, we were in a Broadway hotel whose employees are familiar with the world. When I mentioned these names, the clerk bowed and left us with a smile. Saniette was also of the world; she smiled and went back to bed.

The next morning, remembering their smiles, I thought it advisable to explain my actions again. Not that it was necessary for me to differentiate between the kind of a beating alcohol inspires a temperance-cartoon drunkard to give his hard-working spouse, and the beating I had given Saniette; but, rather, that I found it difficult to illustrate the point I desired to make clear.

"When you think of me, Saniette," I said, "think of two men—myself and the chauffeur within me. This chauffeur is very large and dressed in ugly ready-made clothing. His shoes, soiled from walking about the streets of a great city, are covered with animal ordure and chewing gum. His hands are covered with coarse woollen gloves. On his head is a derby hat.

"The name of this chauffeur is The Desire to Procreate.

"He sits within me like a man in an automobile. His heels are in my bowels, his knees on my heart, his face in my brain. His gloved hands hold me firmly by the tongue; his hands, covered with wool, refuse me speech for the emotions aroused by the face in my brain.

"From within, he governs the sensations I receive through my fingers, eyes, tongue and ears.

"Can you imagine how it feels to have this cloth-covered devil within one? While naked, were you ever embraced by a fully clothed man? Do you remember how his button-covered coat felt, how his heavy shoes felt against your skin? Imagine having this man inside of you, fumbling and fingering your heart and tongue with wool-covered hands, treading your tender organs with stumbling soiled feet."

Because of the phrasing of my complaint, Saniette was able to turn my revenge into a joke. She weathered a second beating with a slow, kind smile.

Saniette represents a distinct type of audience—smart, sophisticated, sensitive yet hardboiled, art-loving frequenters of the little theatres. I am their particular kind of a performer.

Some day I shall obtain my revenge by writing a play for one of their art theatres. A theatre patronized by the discriminating few: art-lovers and book-lovers, school teachers who adore the grass-eating Shaw, sensitive young Jews who adore culture, lending librarians, publisher's assistants, homosexualists and homosexualists' assistants, hard-drinking newpaper men, interior decorators, and the writers of advertising copy.

In this play I shall take my beloved patrons into my confidence and flatter their difference from other theatre-goers. I shall congratulate them on their good taste in preferring Art to animal acts. Then, suddenly, in the midst of some very witty dialogue, the entire cast will walk to the footlights and shout Chekov's advice:

"It would be more profitable for the farmer to raise rats for the granary than for the bourgeois to nourish the artist, who must always be occupied with undermining institutions."

In case the audience should misunderstand and align

itself on the side of the artist, the ceiling of the theatre will be made to open and cover the occupants with tons of loose excrement. After the deluge, if they so desire, the patrons of my art can gather in the customary charming groups and discuss the play.

When he had finished reading, Balso threw the pamphlet away with a sigh. In his childhood, things had been managed differently; besides, shaving had not been permitted before the age of sixteen. Having no alternative, Balso blamed the war, the invention of printing, nineteenth-century science, communism, the wearing of soft hats, the use of contraceptives, the large number of delicatessen stores, the movies, the tabloids, the lack of adequate ventilation in large cities, the passing of the saloon, the soft collar fad, the spread of foreign art, the decline of the western world, commercialism, and, finally, for throwing the artist back on his own personality, the renaissance.

"What is beauty saith my sufferings then?" asked Balso of himself, quoting Marlowe.

As though in answer to his question, he saw standing naked before him a slim young girl busily washing her hidden charms in a public fountain. Through the wood of his brain there buzzed the saw of desire.

She called to him, saying:

"Charge, oh poet, the red-veined flowers of suddenly remembered intimacies—the foliage of memory. Feel, oh poet, the warm knife of thought swift stride and slit in the ready garden.

"Soon the hot seed will come to thwart the knife's progress. The hot seed will come in a joyous burst-birth of reeking undergrowth and swamp forest.

"Walk toward the houses of the city of your memory, oh poet! Houses that are protuberances on the skin of streets—warts, tumors, pimples, corns, nipples, sebaceous cysts, hard and soft chancres.

"Like the gums of false teeth, red are the signs imploring you to enter the game paths lit by iron flowers. Like ants under a new-turned stone, hysterical are the women who run there clad in the silk tights of pleasure, oiled with fish slime. Women whose only delight is to rub the jaded until it becomes irritated and grows new things, pimples of a . . ."

Throwing his arms around her, Balso interrupted her recitation by sticking his tongue into her mouth. But when he closed his eyes to heighten the fun, he felt that he was embracing tweed. He opened them and saw that what he held in his arms was a middle aged woman dressed in a mannish suit and wearing hornrimmed glasses.

"My name is Miss McGeeney," she said. "I am a writer as well as a school teacher. Let's discuss something."

Balso wanted to bash her jaw in, but he found that he could not move. He tried to curse, but could only say: "How interesting. On what are you working?"

"At present I am writing a biography of Samuel Perkins. Stark, clever, disillusioned stuff, with a tenderness devoid of sentiment, yet touched by pity and laughter and irony. Into this book I hope to put the whimsical humor, the kindly satire of a mellow life.

"On the surface *Samuel Perkins: Smeller* [for so I call it] is simply a delightful story for children. The discriminating adult soon discovers, however, that it sprang from the brain of a kindly philosopher, that it is a genial satire on humanity.

"Under the title I intend placing as motto a verse from Juvenal: 'Who is surprised to see a goiter in the Alps? Quis tumidum guttur miratur in Alpibus?' I feel that this quotation strikes the keynote of the work.

"But who is Samuel Perkins, you are probably wondering. Samuel Perkins is the biographer of E. F. Fitzgerald. And who is Fitzgerald? You are of course familiar with D. B. Hobson's life of Boswell. Well, E. F. Fitzgerald is the author of a life of Hobson. The subject of my biography, Samuel Perkins, wrote a life of Fitzgerald.

"Sometime ago, a publisher asked me to write a biography, and I decided to do one of E. F. Fitzgerald. Fortunately, before commencing my study, I met Samuel Perkins who told me that he had written a biography of Fitzgerald the biographer of Hobson the biographer of Boswell. This news did not discourge me, but, on the contrary, made me determine to write a life of Perkins and so become another link in a brilliant literary chain. It seems to me that someone must surely take the hint and write the life of Miss McGreeney, the woman who wrote the biography of the man who wrote the biography of the man who wrote the biography of the man who wrote the biography of Boswell. And that, ad infinitum, we will all go rattling down the halls of time, each one in his or her turn a tin can on the tail of Doctor Johnson.

"But there are other good reasons for writing a life of Perkins. He was a great, if peculiar, genius with a character that lends itself most readily to biography.

"At an age when most men's features are regular, before his personality had been able to elevate any one portion of his physiognomy over the rest, Perkins' face was dominated by his nose. This fact I have ascertained from a collection of early photographs lent me by a profound admirer of Perkins and a fellow practitioner of his art. I refer to Robert Jones, author of a book called *Nosologie*.

"When I met Perkins for the first time, his face reminded me of the body of a man I had known at college. According to gossip current in the girls' dormitory this man abused himself. The source of these rumors lay in the peculiar shape of his body: all the veins, muscles and sinews flowed toward and converged at one point. In a like manner the wrinkles on Perkins' face, the contours of his head, the lines of his brow and chin, seemed to have melted and run into his nose.

"At this first meeting, Perkins said something that was later to prove very illuminating. He quoted Lucretius to the effect that 'his nose was quicker to scent a fetid sore or a rank armpit, than a dog to smell out the hidden sow.' Like most quotations, this one is only partially true. True, that is, of only one stage in Perkins' aesthetic development—the, what I have called quite arbitrarily, excrement period.

"It is possible to explain the powers of Perkins' magnificent sense of smell by the well-known theory of natural compensation. No one who has ever observed the acuteness of touch exhibited by a blind man or the gigantic shoulders of a legless man, will question the fact that Nature compensates for the loss of one attribute by lavishing her bounty on another. And Nature had made in the person of Samuel Perkins another attempt at justice. He was deaf and almost blind; his fingers fumbled stupidly; his mouth was always dry and contained a dull, insensitive tongue. But his nose! His nose was a marvelously sensitive and nice instrument. Nature had concentrated in his sense of smell all the abilities usually distributed among the five senses. She had strengthened this organ and had made it so sensitive that it was able to do duty for all the contact organs. Perkins was able to translate the sensations, sound, sight, taste, and touch, into that of smell. He could smell a chord in D minor, or distinguish between the tone-smell of a violin and that of a viola. He could smell the caress of velvet and the strength of iron. It has been said of him that he could smell an isosceles triangle; I mean that he could apprehend through the sense of smell the principles involved in isosceles triangles.

"In the ability to interpret the functions of one sense in terms of another, he is not alone. A French poet, in a sonnet of the vowels, called the letter I red and the letter U blue. Another symbolist, Father Castel, made a clavichord on which he was able to play melody and harmony by using color. Des Esseintes, Huysmans' hero, used a taste organ on which he composed symphonies for the palate.

"But can you imagine, new-found friend and esteemed poet, how horrible was the predicament of this sensitive and sensuous man forced to interpret the whole external world through conclusions reached by the sense of smell alone? If we have great difficulty in discovering the Real, how much greater must his difficulty have been?

"In my presence, Perkins once called the senses a tread-mill. 'A tread-mill,' he said, 'on which one can go only from the odors of Indian-grass baskets to the sour smells of Africa and the stinks of decay.'

"Rather than a tread-mill, I should call the senses a circle. A step forward along the circumference of a circle is a step nearer the starting place. Perkins went, along the circumference of the circle of his senses, from anticipation to realization, from hunger to satiation, from naïveté to sophistication, from simplicity to perversion. He went [speaking in Perkinsesque] from the smell of new-mown hay to that of musk and vervain [from the primitive to the romantic], and from vervain to sweat and excrement [from the romantic to the realistic]; and, finally, to complete the circuit, from excrement he returned to new-mown hay.

"There is, however, a way out for the artist and Perkins discovered it. The circumference of a circle infinite in size is a straight line. And a man like Perkins is able to make the circle of his sensory experience approach the infinite. He can so qualify the step from simplicity to perversion, for example, that the curve which makes inevitable the return to simplicity is imperceptible.

"One day Perkins told me that he was going to be married. I asked him if he thought his wife would understand him, and whether he thought he could be happy with a woman. He answered no to both questions, and said that he was marrying as an artist. I asked him to explain. He replied that the man who had numbered the smells of the human body and found them to be seven was a fool, unless the number was used in its mystic sense.

"After studying this strange conversation with the master, I discovered his meaning. He had found in the odors of a woman's body, never-ending, ever-fresh variation and change—a world of dreams, seas, roads, forests, textures, colors, flavors, forms. On my questioning him further, he confirmed my interpretation. He told me that he had built from the odors of his wife's body an architecture and an aesthetic, a music and a mathematic. Counterpoint, multiplication, the square of a sensation, the cube root of an experience—all were there. He told me that he had even discovered a politic, a hierarchy of odors: self-government, direct . . . "

By this time, Balso had gotten one of his hands free. He hit Miss McGeeney a terrific blow in the gut and hove her into the fountain.

The wooden horse, Balso realized as he walked on, was inhabited solely by writers in search of an audience, and he
was determined not to be tricked into listening to another
story. If one had to be told, he would tell it.

As he hurried down the seemingly endless corridor, he
began to wonder whether he would ever reach the Anus
Mirabilis again. His feet hurt badly and his head ached.
When he came to a café built into the side of the intestine,
he sat down and ordered a glass of beer. After drinking
the beer, he took a newspaper out of his pocket, put it
over his face and went to sleep.

Balso dreamt that he was a young man again, lurking in
a corner of the Carnegie Hall lobby among the assembled
friends and relatives of music. The lobby was crowded
with the many beautiful girl-cripples who congregate
there because Art is their only solace, most men looking
upon their strange forms with distaste. But it was otherwise with Balso Snell. He likened their disarranged hips,
their short legs, their humps, their splay feet, their wall-
eyes, to ornament. Their strange foreshortenings, hanging
heads, bulging spinesacks, were a delight, for he had ever
preferred the imperfect, knowing well the plainness, the
niceness of perfection.

Spying a beautiful hunchback, he suddenly became sick
with passion. The cripple of his choice looked like some
creature from the depths of the sea. She was tall and
extraordinarily hunched. She was tall in spite of her

enormous hump; but for her dog-leg spine she would have been seven feet high. Moreover, he could be certain that, like all hunchbacks, she was intelligent.

He tipped his hat to her. She smiled and he snatched her from the throng, crying as he took her arm:

"O arabesque, I, Balso Snell, shall replace music in your affections! Your pleasures shall no longer be vicarious. No longer shall you mentally pollute yourself. For me, your sores are like flowers: the new, pink, budlike sores, the full, rose-ripe sores, the sweet, seed-bearing sores. I shall cherish them all. O deviation from the Golden Mean! O out of alignment!"

The Lepi [for so did he instantly dub her] opened her mouth to reply and exhibited one hundred and forty-four exquisite teeth in rows of four.

"Balso," she said, "you are a villian. Do you love as do all villains?"

"No," he answered, "I love only this." As he spoke, he laid his cool white hands upon her beautiful, hydrocephalic forehead. Then, bending over her enormous hump, he kissed her full on the brow.

Feeling his lips on her forehead, Janey Davenport, [the Lepi] gazed out over the blue waves of the Mediterranean and felt the delight of being young, rich, beautiful. No-one had ever before forgotten her strange shape long enough to realize how beautiful her soul was. She had never before known the thrill of being subdued by a male from a different land from that of her dreams. Now she had found a wonderful poet; now she knew the thrill she had never known before . . . had found it in the strength of this young and tall, strangely wise man, caught like herself in the meshes of the greatest net human hearts can know: Love.

Balso took her home and, in the hallway of her house, tried to seduce her. She allowed him one kiss, then broke away. From her lips—overhung by a moist eye and under-hung by a heaving embonpoint—there came, "Love is a strange thing, is it not, Balso Snell?" He was afraid to laugh; he knew that if he even smiled the jig would be up. "Love," she said, "is beautiful. You, Balso, do not love. Love is sacred. How can you kiss if you do not love?" When he began to unbutton, she said with a desperately gay smile: "Would you want some one to ask of your sister what you ask of me? So this is why you invited me to dinner? I pre-fer music."

He made another attempt, but she fended him off. "Love," she began again, "Love, with me, Mr. Snell, is sacred. I shall never debase love, or myself, or the mem-ory of my mother, in a hallway. Act your education, Mr. Snell. Tumbling in hallways at my age! How can you? After all, there are the eternal verities, not to speak of the janitor. And besides, we were never properly introduced."

After half an hour's sparring, he managed to warm her up a bit. She held him to her tightly for a second, capsized her eyeballs, and said: "If you only loved me, Balso. If you only loved me." He looked her in the eye, stroked her hump, kissed her brow, protesting desperately: "But I do love you, Janey. I do. I do. I swear it. I must have you. I must! I must!" She shoved him away with a sad yet deter-mined smile. "First you will have to prove your love as did the knights of old."

"I'm ready," Balso cried. "What would you have me do?"

"Come inside and I'll tell you."

Balso followed her into the apartment and sat down be-side her on a couch.

"I want you to kill a man called Beagle Darwin," she said with great firmness. "He betrayed me. In this hump on my back I carry his child. After you have killed him, I shall yield up my pink and white body to you, and then commit suicide."

"A bargain," Balso said. "Give me but your stocking to wear around my hat and I'm off to earn the prize."

"Not so fast, my gallant; first I must explain a few things to you.

"After listening to Beagle Darwin recite some of his poetry, I slept with him one night while my folks were visiting friends in Plainfield, New Jersey. Unfamiliar as I was with the wiles of men, I believed him when he told me that he loved me and wanted to take me to Paris to live in an artistic studio. I was very happy until I received the following letter."

Here the Lepi went to a bureau and took out two letters, one of which she gave Balso to read.

Darling Janey:

You persist in misunderstanding me. Please understand this: It is for your own good that I am refusing to take you to Paris, as I am firmly convinced that such a trip can only result in your death.

Here is the way in which you would die:

In your pajamas, Janey, you sit near the window and listen to the gay clatter of Paris traffic. The highpitched automobile horns make of every day a holiday. You are miserable.

You tell yourself: Oh, the carnival crowds are always hurrying past my window. I'm like an old actor mumbling Macbeth as he fumbles in the garbage can outside the theatre of his past triumphs. Only I'm not old; I'm young. Young, and I never had any triumphs to mumble over; my only triumphs were those I dreamed of having. I'm Janey Davenport, pregnant, unmarried, unloved, lonely, watching the laughing crowds hurry past her window.

I don't fit into life. I don't fit into his life. He only tolerates me for my body. He only wants one thing from me, and I want, oh how I want, love.

The ridiculous, the ridiculous, all day long he talks of nothing else but how ridiculous this, that, or the other thing is. And he means me. I am absurd. He is never satisfied with calling other people ridiculous, with him everything is ridiculous—himself, me. Of course I can laugh at Mother with him, or at the Hearth; but why must my own mother and home be ridiculous? I can laugh at Hobey, Joan, but I don't want to laugh at myself. I'm tired of laugh, laugh, laugh. I want to retain some portion of myself unlaughed at. There is something in me that I won't laugh at. I won't. I'll laugh at the outside world all he wants me to, but I won't, I don't want to laugh at my inner world. It's all right for him to say: "Be hard! Be an intellectual! Think, don't feel!" But I want to be soft. I want to feel. I don't want to think. I feel blue when I think. I want to keep a hard, outside surface towards the world, and a soft, inner side for him. And I want him to do the same, so that we can be secure in each other's love. But with his rotten, ugly jokes he keeps me at arm's length just when I want to be confiding and tender. When I show him my soft side he laughs. I don't want to be always on my guard against his laughter. There are times when I want to put down my armor. I am tired of eternally bearing armor against the world. Love is a merging, not an occasion for intellectual warfare. I want to enjoy my emotions. I want, sometimes, to play the child, and to make love like a child—tenderly, confidingly, prettily. I'm sick of his taunts.

Pregnant, unmarried, and he won't marry me. If I ask him to, he will laugh his terrible horse-laugh: "Well, my little bohemian, you want to get out of it, do you? Life, however, is Life; and the Realities are the Realities. You can't have your cake and eat it too, you know." He'll tell his friends the story as a joke—one of his unexplainable jokes. All his smug-faced friends will laugh at me, especially the Paige girl.

They don't like me; I don't fit in. All my life I have been a misfit—misunderstood. The carnival crowds are always hurrying past my window. As a kid, I never liked to play in the streets with the other kids; I always wanted to stay in the house and read a book. Since my father's death, I have no one to go to with my misery. He was always willing to understand and comfort me. Oh, how I want to be understood by someone who really loves me. Mother, like Beagle, always laughs at me. If they want to be kind it is, "You silly goose!" If they are angry, "Don't be an idiot." Only father was sympathetic, and he is dead. I wish I were dead.

Joan Higgins would know what to do if she were in my position—pregnant and unmarried. Joan fits into the kind of a life he and his friends lead better than I do. Like the time Joan said she had gone back to live with Hobey because it was such a bore looking for healthy men to sleep with. Joan warned me against him; she said he wasn't my kind. I thought him just my kind, sad and a poet. He is sad, but with a nasty sadness—all jeers for his own sadness. "It's the war. Everybody is sad nowadays. Great stuff, pessimism." Still he is sad; if he would only stop acting we could be very happy together. I want so much to comfort him—mother him.

Joan's advice would probably be for me to make him marry me. How he would howl. "Make an honest girl of you, eh?"

You can see the Café Carcas from the window. You are living in the Rue de la Grande Chaumiere, at the Hotel Liberia.

Why don't I fit in well at the Carcas? Joan would go big there. Why don't they like me? I'm as good looking as she is, and as clever. It's because I don't let myself go the way she does. Well, I don't want to. There is something fine in me that won't let me degrade myself.

You see me come out of the café, laughing and waving my arms.

I hope he comes upstairs.

You see me turn, and come towards the hotel.

Just as soon as he comes in I'll tell him I'm pregnant. I'll tell him in a matter-of-fact voice—casually. As long as I keep my tone casual he won't be able to laugh.

"Hello darling, how are you this morning?"
"All right. Beagle, je suis enceinte."
"You're what?"
[Oh, damn my pronunciation, I spoilt it.] "I'm pregnant." Despite your desire to appear casual you let a note of heartbreak into your voice. You droop.
"We'll have a party tonight and celebrate." I leave the room, shutting the door behind me, carefully.
Perhaps he'll never come back . . . You run to the window—sick. You sit down and prepare to indulge your misery. Your misery, your misery—you roll, you grovel in it. I'm pregnant! I'm pregnant! I'm pregnant! You force the rhythm of this cry into your blood. After the first moments of hysterical anguish are over, you wrap your predicament around you, snuggling into it, letting it cover you completely like a blanket. Your big trouble shelters you from a host of minor troubles. You are so miserable.

You remember that "life is a prison without bars," and think of suicide.

No one ever listens to me when I talk of suicide. The night I woke up in bed with him, it was no different. He thought I was joking when I said that I had frightened myself by brooding on death. But I told the truth. Death and suicide are never far from my thoughts. I said that death is like putting on a wet bathing suit. Now death seems warm and friendly. No, death is still like putting on a wet suit—shivery.

If I do it, I won't leave a note behind for him to laugh at. Just end it, that's all. No matter how I word a farewell note he will find something to laugh at—something to show his friends as a joke . . .

Mother knows I'm living with a man in Paris. Sophie wrote that everybody is talking about me. If I were to go home—even if I were not pregnant—mother would make an awful stink. I don't want to go back to the States: a long dull trip followed by a long dull life teaching elementary school.

What can I expect from him? He'll want me to have an abortion. They say that on account of the decreasing birth rate it is hard to get a competent doctor to do the operation. The French police are very strict. If the doctor killed me . . .

If I kill myself, I kill my body. I don't want to destroy my body; it is a good body—soft, white, and kind to me— a beautiful, happy body. If he were a true poet he would love me for my body's beauty; but he is like all men; he wants only one thing. Soon my body will be swollen and clumsy. The milk spoils the shape of a woman's breasts after an abortion. When my body becomes ugly, he will hate me. I once hoped that having a child would draw him closer to me—make him love me as a mother. But mother for him is always Mammy: a popular Broadway ballad, Mammy, Mammy, my old Kentucky Home, put it all together, it spells Mother. He doesn't see that Mother can mean shelter, love, intimacy. Oh, how much I want, I need, love.

If I wanted to make a squawk, mother would force him to marry me; but she would scold terribly and make a horrible scene. I'm too tired and sick to go through with a shotgun wedding.

Maybe I passed my period because of the wine—no, I know. Where did I read, "In my belly there is a tangled forest of arms and legs." It sounds like his stuff. When he left, he said he'd give a party tonight in honor of the occasion. I know what kind of a party it will be. He'll get drunk and make a speech: "Big with child, great with young—let me toast your gut; my dear. Here's to the pup! Waiters, stand erect while I toast my heir." He and his friends will expect me to join in the sport—to be a good sport.

He claims that the only place to commit suicide is on Chekov's grave. The Seine is also famous for suicide: "'midst the bustle of 'Gay Paree'—suicide." "She killed herself in Paris." There is something tragic in the very thought. French windows make it easy; all you have to do is open the window and walk out. Every window over the third floor is a door into heaven. When I arrive there I can plead my belly—oh, how bitterly cruel the jest is. "Jest?" He would correct me—"not 'jest,' my dear, but joke; never, never say 'jest.'"

Oh, how miserable I am. I need love; I can't live without someone to treasure and comfort me. If I jumped from the third floor I might cripple myself—lucky this room is on the fourth. Lucky? [Animals never commit suicide.]

And mother—what would mother say? Mother would

feel worse about my being unmarried than about my death. I could leave a note asking him, as a final favor, to write her and say that we were married. He would forget to write.

When I'm dead, I'll be out of it all. Mother, Beagle— they will leave me alone. But I can't blame my trouble on him. I got myself into this mess. I went to his room after he acted decently in mine. I was jealous of Joan; she had so much fun going to men's rooms, and all that sort of thing. How childish Joan and her follies seem to me now.

When I'm dead the whole world as far as I am concerned—Beagle, mother—will be dead also. Or aussi: I came to Paris to learn French. I certainly learnt French. I wasn't even able to tell him in French without turning my trouble into a joke.

What love and a child by the man I loved once meant to me—and to live in Paris. If he should come back suddenly and catch me like this, brooding at the window, he'd say: "A good chance for you to kill two birds with one stone, my dear; but remember, an egg in the belly is worth more than a bird in the bush." What a pig he is! He thinks I haven't the nerve to kill myself. He patronizes me as though I were a child. "Suicide," he says, "is a charming affectation on the part of a young Russian, but in you, dear Janey, it is absurd."

You scream with irritation: "I'm serious! I am! I am! I don't want to live! I'm miserable! I don't want to live!"

I'm only teasing myself with thoughts of suicide at an open window. I know I won't do it. Mother will call me away: "Go away from that window—fool! You'll catch your death-cold or fall out—clumsy!"

At the word "clumsy" you fall to your death in the gutter below the window.

Horrible, eh? Yes, Janey, it is a suicide's grave that I saved you from when I refused to take you to Paris.

Yours,

Beagle

When Balso had finished reading, she handed him the other letter.

Darling Janey:

You did not take offence, I hope, at my letter. Please believe me when I say that I tried to make my treatment of your suicide as impersonal as possible. I did my best to keep the description of both our characters scientific and just. If I treated you savagely, I treated myself no gentler. It is true that I concentrated on you, but only because it was your suicide. In this letter I shall try to show, and so even the score, how I would have received your death.

You once said to me that I talk like a man in a book. I not only talk, but think and feel like one. I have spent my life in books; literature has deeply dyed my brain its own color. This literary coloring is a protective one—like the brown of the rabbit or the checks of the quail—making it impossible for me to tell where literature ends and I begin.

I start where I left off in my last letter:

As Janey's half-naked body crashed into the street, the usual crowds were hurrying to lunch from the Academies Colorossa and Grande Chaumiere; the concierge was coming out of the hotel's side door. In order to avoid running over her body, the driver of a cab coming from the Rue Notre Dame des Champs and going toward the Square de la Grande Chaumiere, brought his machine to a stop with screaming brakes. The concierge, on seeing the cab stop suddenly, one wheel over the body of a tenant of his, ran up, caught the chauffeur by the arm, and called loudly for the police. No one had seen her fall but the driver of the cab; he, bursting with rage, called the concierge an idiot, and pointed to the open window from which she had jumped. A crowd gathered around the chauffeur and shouted at him angrily. A policeman arrived. He, too, refused to believe the cab-driver, although he noticed that the dead girl was in her pajamas. "What would she be doing in the street in her night-clothes if she hadn't fallen from the window?" He shrugged his shoulders: "These American art students."

Beagle, on his way to the Café Carcas for a drink, turned to see where so many people were running. He saw the gesticulating group around the cab and went back, grateful for any diversion on what had been such a dull morning. As he joined them he kept thinking of Janey's announcement. "I'm pregnant." It reminded him of another announcement of hers. "It's about time I took a lover." "I'm pregnant" demanded for an answer, Life, just as "It's about time I took a lover" had been worthy of no less a reply than Love. She made a habit of these startling declarations: a few words, but freighted with meaning.

He knew what "I'm pregnant" meant; it meant canvassing his friends for the whereabouts of a doctor willing to perform the operation and writing frantic letters to the States for the necessary money. Through it all, Janey, having thrown the responsibility on him, would sit in one corner of the room: "Do with me what you will"—the groaning, patient, all-suffering, all-knowing, what has to be will be, beast of many burdens.

As he pushed into the crowd, someone told him a girl had been killed. He looked where the chauffeur was pointing and saw the open window of their room. Then he saw

Janey under the cab; he could not see her face, but he recognized her pajamas.

This was indeed a solution. The problem had been solved for him with a vengeance. He turned away and hurried up the street, afraid of being recognized. It had become impossible for him to take his drink at the Carcas. If he went there some friend would surely come to him with the news: "Beagle! Beagle! Janey has killed herself." He wanted to go somewhere and prepare a reply. "Here today and gone tomorrow" would never do, even at the Carcas.

He went past the Carcas up the Rue Delambre to the Avenue de Maine. On this street he went into a café hardly ever visited by Americans and sat down at a table in the corner of an inside room. He called for some cognac and asked himself:

Of what assistance could I have been? Should I have gone down on my knees in the street and wept over her dead body? Torn my hair? Called on the Deity? Or should I gave gone calmly up to the policeman and said: "I'm her husband. Allow me to accompany you to the morgue."

He ordered another cognac—Beagle Darwin the Destroyer. He pulled his hat down over his eyes and tossed off his drink.

She did it because she was pregnant. I would have married her, the fool. I hurt her when I made believe I didn't understand her French. "Je suis enceinte." My "what" was one of the astonishment, not the "what" of interrogation. No, it was not. You said "what" in order to humiliate her. What is the purpose of all your harping on petty affectations? Why this continual irritation at the sight of other peoples' stupidities? What of your own stupidities and affectations? Why is it impossible for you to understand, except in terms of art, her action? She killed herself because she was afraid to face her troubles—an abortion or the birth of a bastard. Absurd; she never asked you to marry her. You do not understand.

He crouched over his drink, Tiger Darwin, his eyes half shut—desperate.

I wonder if she was able to avoid generalizing before she killed herself. I am sure it was not trouble, that was uppermost in her mind, but the rag-tag of some "philosophy." Although I did my best to laugh away finita la comedia, I am certain that some such catch-word of disillusion was in her mouth when she turned the trick. She probably decided that Love, Life, Death, all could be contained in an epigram: "The things which are of value in Life are empty and rotten and trifling; Love is but a flitting shadow, a lure, a gimcrack, a kickshaw. And Death?—bah! What, then, is there still detaining you in this vale of tears?" Can it be that the only thing that bothers me in a statement of this sort is the wording? Or is it because there is something arty about suicide? Suicide: Werther, the Cosmic Urge, the Soul, the Quest, and Otto Greenbaum, Phil Beta Kappa, Age seventeen— Life is unworthy of him; and Haldington Knape, Oxford, author, man-about-town, big game hunter—Life is too tiresome; and Terry Kornflower, poet, no hat, shirt open to the navel—Life is too crude; and Janey Davenport, pregnant, unmarried, jumps from a studio window in Paris —Life is too difficult. O. Greenbaum, H. Knape, T. Kornflower, J. Davenport, all would agree that "Life is but the span from womb to tomb; a sigh, a smile; a chill, a fever; a throe of pain, a spasm of volupty: then a gasping for breath, and the comedy is over, the song is ended, ring down the curtain, the clown is dead."

The clown is dead; the curtain is down. And when I say clown, I mean you. After all, aren't we all . . . aren't we all clowns? Of course, I know it's old stuff; but what difference does that make? Life *is* a stage; and *we* are clowns. What is more tragic than the role of clown? What more filled with all the essentials of great art?—pity and irony. Get it? The thousands of sweating, laughing, grimacing, jeering animals out front—you have just set them in the aisles, when in comes a messenger. Your wife has run away with the boarder, your son has killed a man, the baby has cancer. Or maybe you ain't married. Coming from the bathroom, you discover that you have gonorrhoea, or you get a telegram that your mother is dead, or your father, or your sister, or your brother. Now get the picture. Outside, after your turn, the customers are hollering and screaming: "Do your stuff, kid! We want Beagle! Let's have Beagle! He's a wow!" The clowns down front are laughing, whistling, belching, crying, sweating, and eating peanuts. And you—you are back-stage, hiding in the shadow of an old prop. Clutching your bursting head with both hands, you hear nothing but the dull roar of your misfortunes. Slowly there filters through your clenched fingers the cries of your brother clowns. Your first thought is to rush out there and cut your throat before their faces with a last terrific laugh. But soon you are out front again doing your stuff, the same superb Beagle: dancing, laughing, singing—*acting*. Finally the curtain comes down, and, in your dressing room before the mirror, you make the faces that won't come off with the grease paint—the faces you will never make down front.

Beagle ordered another cognac and washed it down with a small beer. The saucers had begun to pile up before him on the table.

Well, Janey's death is a joke. A young, unmarried woman on discovering herself to be pregnant commits suicide. A very old and well-known way out of a very old and stale predicament. The moth and the candle, the fly and the spider, the butterfly and the rain, the clown and the curtain, all could be cited as having prepared one [oh how tediously!] for her suicide.

Another cognac! After this cognac, he would go to the Café Carcas and wait for a friend to bring him news of Janey's death.

How shall I receive the devastating news? In order to arouse no adverse criticism, it will be necessary for me to bear in mind that I come of an English-speaking race and therefore am cold, calm, collected, almost stolid, in the face of calamity. And, as the death is that of a very intimate friend, it is important that I show, in some subtle way, that I am hard hit for all my pretence of coldness. Or perhaps because the Carcas is full of artists, I can refuse to stop dreaming, refuse to leave my ivory tower, refuse to disturb that brooding white bird, my spirit. A wave of the hand: "Yes, really. You don't say so?—quite dead." Or I can play one of my favorite roles, be the "Buffoon of the New Eternities" and cry: "Death, what is it? Life, what is it? Life is of course the absence of Death; and Death merely the absence of Life." But I might get into an argument unbecoming one who is lamenting the loss of a loved one. For the sake of the waiters, I will be a quiet, sober, gentle, umbrella-carrying Mr. B. Darwin, and out of a great sadness sob: "Oh, my darling, why did you do it? Oh why?" Or, best of all, like Hamlet, I will feign madness; for if they discover what lies in my heart they will lynch me.

MESSENGER

"Beagle! Beagle! Janey has fallen from the window and is no more."

PATRONS, WAITERS, ETC., AT THE CAFÉ CARCAS

"The girl you lived with is dead."

"Poor Janey. Poor Beagle. Terrible, terrible death."

"And so young she was, and so beautiful . . . in the cold street she lay."

B. HAMLET DARWIN

"Bromius! Iacchus! Son of Zeus!"

PATRONS, WAITERS, ETC.

"Don't you understand, man? The girl you lived with is dead. Your sweetheart is dead. She has killed herself. She is dead!"

B. HAMLET DARWIN

"Bromius! Iacchus! Son of Zeus!"

PATRONS, WAITERS, ETC.

"He's drunk."

"Greek gods!—does he think we don't know he's a Methodist?"

"This is no time for blasphemy!"

"A little learning goes to the heads of fools."

"Yes, drink deep of the Pierian spring or . . ."

"Very picturesque though, 'Bromius! Iacchus!' very picturesque."

B. HAMLET DARWIN

" 'O esca vermium! O massa pulveris!' Where is the rich Dives? He who was always eating? He is no longer even eaten."

PATRONS, WAITERS, ETC.

"A riddle! A riddle!"

"He is looking for a friend."

"He has lost something. Tell him to look under the table."

MESSENGER

"He means the worms have eaten Dives; and that, in their turn dead, the worms have been eaten by other worms."

B. HAMLET DARWIN

"Or quick tell me where has gone Samson?—strongest of men. He is no longer even weak. And where, oh tell me, where is the beautiful Appollon? He is no longer even ugly. And where are the snows of yesteryear? And where is Tom Giles? Bill Taylor? Jake Holtz? In other words, 'Here today and gone tomorrow.'"

MESSENGER

"Yes, what he says is but too true. An incident such as the sad demise we are now considering makes one stop 'midst the hustle-bustle of our work-a-day world to ponder the words of the poet who says we are 'nourriture des vers!' Continue, dear brother in sorrow, we attend your every word."

B. HAMLET DARWIN

"I shall begin all over again, folks.

"While I sit laughing with my friends, a messenger stalks into the café. He cries: "Beagle! Beagle! Janey has killed herself!' I jump up, white as a sheet of paper, let us say, and shriek in anguish: 'Bromius! Iacchus! Son of Zeus!' You then demand why I call so loudly on Dionysius. I go into my routine.

"Dionysius! Dionysius! I call on the wine-god because his begetting and birth were so different from Janey's, so different from yours, so different from mine. I call on Dionysius in order to explain the tragedy. A tragedy that is not alone Janey's, but one that is the tragedy of all of us.

"Who among us can boast that he was born three times, as was Dionysius?—once from the womb of 'hapless Semele,' once from the thigh of Zeus, and once from the flames. Or who can say, like Christ, that he was born of a virgin? Or who can even claim to have been born as was Gargantua? Alas! none of us. Yet it is necessary for us to compete—as it was necessary for Janey to compete—with Dionysius the thrice born, Christ son of God, Gargantua born 'midst a torrent of tripe at a most memorable party. You hear the thunder, you see the lightning, you smell the forests, you drink wine—and you attempt to be as was Christ, Dionysius, Gargantua! You who were born from the womb, covered with slime and foul blood, 'midst cries of anguish and suffering.

"At your birth, instead of the Three Kings, the Dove, the Star of Bethlehem, there was only old Doctor Haasenschweitz who wore rubber gloves and carried a towel over his arm like a waiter.

"And how did the lover, your father, come to his beloved? [After a warm day in the office he had seen two dogs in the street.] Did he come in the shape of a swan, a bull, or a shower of gold? No! But with his pants unsupported by braces, came he from the bath-room." . . .

B. Hamlet Darwin towered over his glass of cognac, and, in the theatre of his mind, over a cringing audience —tempestuous, gallant, headstrong, lovable Beagle Dionysius Hamlet Darwin. Up into his giant heart there welled a profound feeling of love for humanity. He choked with emotion as he realized the truth of his observations. Terrible indeed was the competition in which his hearers spent their lives; a competition that demanded their being more than animals.

He raised his hand as though to bless them, and the customers and waiters were silent. Gently, yet with a sense of mighty love, he murmured, "Ah my children." Then, sweeping the Café Carcas with tear-dimmed, eagle's eyes, he cried: "Yet, ah yet, are you expected to compete with Christ whose father is God, with Dionysius whose father is God; you who were Janey Davenport, or one conceived in an offhand manner on a rainy afternoon."

"Cognac! Cognac!"

After building up his tear-jerker routine for a repeat, he blacked out and went into his juggling for the curtain. He climaxed the finale by keeping in the air an Ivory Tower, a Still White Bird, the Holy Grail, the Nails, the Scourge, the Thorns, and a piece of the True Cross.

Yours,

Beagle

"Well, what do you think of them?"

Balso awoke and saw Miss McGeeney, the biographer of Samuel Perkins, sitting beside him at the café table.

"Think of what?"

"The two letters you just read," Miss McGeeney said impatiently. "They form part of a novel I'm writing in the manner of Richardson. Give me your candid opinion: do you think the epistolary style too old-fashioned?"

Refreshed by the nap he had taken, Balso examined his interrogator with interest. She was a fine figure of a woman. He wanted to please her and said:

"A stormy wind blows through your pages, sweeping

the reader breathless . . . witchery and madness. Comparable to George Bernard Shaw. It is a drama of passion that has all the appeal of wild living and the open road. Comparable to George Bernard Shaw. There's magic in its pages, and warm strong sympathy for an alien race."

"Thank you," she said with precision.

How gracious is a woman grateful, thought Balso. He felt young again: the heel of a loaf, a piece of cheese, a bottle of wine and an apple. Clear speakers, naked in the sun. Young students: and the days are very full, and the nights burst with excitement, and life is a torrent roaring.

"Oh!" Balso exclaimed, carried away by these memories of his youth. "Oh!" His mouth formed an O with lips torn angry in laying duck's eggs from a chicken's rectum.

"Oh, what?" Miss McGeeney was obviously annoyed.

"Oh, I loved a girl once. All day she did nothing but place bits of meat on the petals of flowers. She choked the rose with butter and cake crumbs; soiling the crispness of its dainty petals with gravy and cheese. She wanted the rose to attract flies, not butterflies or bees. She wanted to make of her garden a . . ."

"Balso! Balso! Is it you?" cried Miss McGeeney, spilling what was left of his beer, much to the disgust of the waiter who hovered near.

"Balso! Balso! Is it you?" she cried again before he could answer. "Don't you recognize me? I'm Mary. Mary McGeeney, your old sweetheart."

Balso realized that she was indeed Mary. Changed, alas! but with much of the old Mary left, particularly about the eyes. No longer was she dry and stick-like, but a woman, warmly moist.

They sat and devoured each other with looks until the waiter suggested that they leave as he wanted to close the place and go home.

They left arm-in-arm, walking as in a dream. Balso did

the steering and they soon found themselves behind a thick clump of bushes. Miss McGeeney lay down on her back with her hands behind her head and her knees wide apart. Balso stood over her and began a speech the intent of which was obvious.

"First," he said, "let us consider the political aspect. You who talk of Liberty and cling to the protection of Dogma in the face of Life and the Army of Unutterable Physical Law, cast, I say, cast free the anchors, let go the moorings of your desires! Let to the breezes flap the standard of your revolt!

"Also we must consider the philosophical aspects of the proposed act. Nature has lent you for a brief time a few organs capable of giving pleasure. Among these are to be listed the sexual ones. The organs of sex offer in reward for their intelligent use a very intense type of pleasure. Pleasure, it is necessary to admit, is the only good. It is only reasonable to say that if pleasure is desirable—and who besides a few fanatics say it is not?—one should get all the pleasure possible. First it is important to dissociate certain commonplace ideas. As a thinking person, as an individualist—and you are both of these, are you not, love?—it is necessary to dissociate the idea of pleasure from that of generation. Furthermore, it is necessary to disregard one's unreasonable moral training. Sex, not marriage, is a sacrament. You admit it? Then why allow an ancient, inherited code to foist on you, a thinking being, the old, outmoded strictures? Sexual acts are not sins, errors, faults, weaknesses. The sexual acts give pleasure, and pleasure is desirable. So come, Mary, let us have some fun.

"And for the sake of Art, Mary. You desire to write, do you not, love? And you must admit that without knowing what all the shooting is about, a sincere artist is badly handicapped. How can you portray men if you have never known a man? How can you read and understand, see and understand, without ever having known the divine excitement? How can you hope to motivate a theft, a murder, a rape, a suicide, convincingly? And are you ever out of themes? In my bed, love, you will find new themes, new interpretations, new experiences. You will be able to judge for yourself whether love is only three minutes of rapture followed by a feeling of profound disgust, or the all-consuming fire, the divine principle, a foretaste of the joys of heaven? Come, Mary McGeeney, to bed and a new world.

"And now, finally, we come to the Time-argument. Do not confuse what I shall say under this head with the theories so much in vogue among the metaphysicians and physicists, those weavers of the wind. My 'Time' is that of the poets. In a little while, love, you will be dead; that is my burden. In a little while, we all will be dead. Golden lads and chimney-sweeps, all dead. And when dying, will you be able to say, I turn down an empty glass, having drunk to the full, lived to the full? Is it not madness to deny life? Hurry! Hurry! for all is soon over. Blown, O rose! in the morning, thou shalt fade ere noon. Do you realize the tune the clock is playing? The seconds, how they fly! All is soon over! All is soon over! Let us snatch, while yet we may, in this brief span, whose briefness merely gilds the bubble so soon destroyed, some few delights. Have you thought of the grave? O love! have you thought of the grave and of the change that shall come over your fair body? Your most beautiful bride—though now she be pleasant and sweet to the nose—will be damnably mouldy a hundred years hence. O how small a part of time they share, that are so wonderous sweet and fair. Ah, make the most of what we yet may spend before we too into the dust descend. Into the dust, Mary! Thy sweet plenty, in the dust. I tremble, I burn for thy sweet embrace. Be not miserly with thy white flesh. Give your gracious body, for such a short time lent you. Give, for in the giving you shall receive and still have what you give. Only time can rob you of your flesh, I cannot. And time will rob you—it will, it will! And those who husbanded the golden grain, and those who flung it to the wind like rain . . ."

Here Balso threw himself to the ground beside his beloved.

How did she receive him? At first, by saying no.

No. No! Innocent, confused. Oh Balso! Oh Balso! with pictures of the old farm house, old pump, old folks at home, and the old oaken bucket—ivy over all.

Sir! Stamping her tiny foot—imperative, irate. Sir, how dare you, sir! Do you presume? Down, Rover, I say down! The prying thumbs of insolent chauffeurs. The queen chooses. Elizabeth of England, Catherine of Russia, Faustina of Rome.

These two noes graded into two yes-and-noes.

No . . . Oh . . . Oh, no. Eyes aswim with tears. Voice throaty, husky with repressed passion. Oh, how sweet, sweetheart, sweetheart, sweetheart. Oh, I'm melting. My very bones are liquid. I'll swoon if you don't leave me alone. Leave me alone, I'm dizzy. No . . . No! You beast!

No: No, Balso, not tonight. No, not tonight. No! I'm sorry, Balso, but not tonight. Some other time, perhaps yes, but not tonight. Please be a dear, not tonight. Please!

But Balso would not take no for an answer, and he soon obtained the following yeses:

Allowing hot breath to escape from between moist, open lips: eyes upset, murmurs love. Tiger skin on divan. Spanish shawl on grand piano. Altar of Love. Church and Brothel. Odors of Ind and Afric. There's Egypt in your eyes. Rich, opulent love; beautiful, tapestried love; oriental, perfumed love.

Hard-bitten. Casual. Smart. Been there before. I've had policemen. No trace of a feminine whimper. Decidedly revisiting well-known, well-plowed ground. No new trees, wells, or even fences.

Desperate for life. Live! Experience! Live one's own. Your body is an instrument, an organ or a drum. Harmony. Order. Breasts. The apple of my eye, the pear of my abdomen. What is life without love? I burn! I ache! Hurrah!

Moooompitcher yaaaah. Oh I never hoped to know the passion, the sensuality hidden within you—yes, yes. Drag me down into the mire, drag. Yes! And with your hair the lust from my eyes brush. Yes . . . Yes . . . Ooh! Ah!

The miracle was made manifest. The Two became One. The One that is all things and yet no one of them: the priest and the god, the immolation, the sacrificial rite, the libation offered to ancestors, the incantation, the sacrificial egg, the altar, the ego and the alter ego, as well as the father, the child, and the grandfather of the universe, the mystic doctrine, the purification, the syllable "Om," the path, the master, the witness, the receptacle, the Spirit of Public School 186, the last ferry that leaves for Weehawken at seven.

His body broke free of the bard. It took on a life of its own; a life that knew nothing of the poet Balso. Only to death can this release be likened—to the mechanics of decay. After death the body takes command; it performs the manual of disintegration with a marvelous certainty. So now, his body performed the evolutions of love with a like sureness.

In this activity, Home and Duty, Love and Art, were forgotten.

An army moved in his body, an eager army of hurrying sensations. These sensations marched at first methodically and then hysterically, but always with precision. The army of his body commenced a long intricate drill, a long involved ceremony. A ceremony whose ritual unwound and manoeuvred itself with the confidence and training of chemicals acting under the stimulus of a catalytic agent.

His body screamed and shouted as it marched and uncoiled; then, with one heaving shout of triumph, it fell back quiet.

The army that a moment before had been thundering in his body retreated slowly—victorious, relieved.